D1470170

Winter of the Crystal Dances

Angela Dorsey

Winter of the Crystal Dances

Winter of the Crystal Dances
Copyright: Text © 2010 by Angela Dorsey
www.angeladorsey.com
The author asserts her moral right to be identified as the author of the
work in relation to all such rights as are granted by the autor to the
publisher under the terms and conditions of this agreement.
Original title: As above
Cover and inside illustrations: © Jennifer Bell
Cover layout: © Stabenfeldt A/S

Typeset by Roberta L Melzl
Editor: Bobbie Chase
Printed in Germany, 2009

ISBN: 978-1-934983-38-6

Stabenfeldt, Inc.
225 Park Avenue South
New York, NY 10003
www.pony4kids.com

Available exclusively through PONY.

cold nips ears
bites sides
snaps trees
can't hide

crusts snow
covers grass
thickens water
frozen fast

invades lungs
mists breath
shivers skin
makes death

Luckily, I stayed up late that night, reading by lantern light until my eyes burned. Yeah, you guessed right – we don't have electricity. When I finally accepted that the book was too long to finish before morning, I closed it grudgingly.

Loonie, our ancient German Shepherd – she's almost thirteen, like me – raised her head and whined, sensing I was about to desert her. I scratched behind her ears, then picked up the lantern and carried it into the second room of our tiny cabin, the bedroom I share with my mom.

The cold floor bit at my feet and the air wasn't much warmer, even though the door was wide open to the front room where our wood stove belched out heat. I jumped beneath my big fluffy quilt and snuggled in, then peeked out to blow out the lantern. Mom slept on undisturbed. Moonlight splashed through the small window above her bed and coated her blankets with liquid silver. Her face was peaceful in the glow. She'd never know how late I stayed up.

I closed my eyes and began my own trip to dreamland.

Hunger and pain rumble into my body like an avalanche. My legs are raw and bloody, my stomach an

*empty cavern. I long to drop into the soft snow, I am so
weak and tired, and so very, very cold – but death lies
there. And worse. I can face my own death. But the death
of my foal – and he will die without me – I cannot bear.*

The mustangs were near. And they were starving.

Okay, time out. Let me explain before you think I'm
totally whacked. I have a "gift." I hear horses. Actually,
maybe hear is the wrong word. It's more like I can feel
them, and with some horses, the ones who think more
abstractly, I can translate my impressions into words.
Basically, when a horse steps into the river, I sense
what it senses – wet, cold, the current pushing – and
though I'm not in the river, or near a river, the feeling of
stepping into a river is completely real to me. Usually it's
not quite as strong as things I feel myself as a human –
unless the feeling is panicky or desperate. Then it takes
over. Completely. That's only happened a few times, but
believe me, it's not remotely cool. It's terrifying.

Only Rusty, my gray gelding, knows about my weird
talent, if it can even be called a talent. Rusty and I can
even talk. He's picked up a bit of language and grammar.
I know that sounds crazy but it's true. And in turn,
I've learned how to better interpret horse thoughts by
speaking with him. I've never talked to any other horse
but Rusty – well, except once, and it ended very badly
for the horse. She was one of the mustangs. Her name
was Willow, and – I'm sorry. I can't go there. I thought I
could, but I can't. Let's leave it at that.

No humans know of my ability. I learned to keep quiet
about it because of my mom. I tried to tell her once, a

7

long time ago when she said she believed in magic. I don't know what kind of magic she was talking about because when I told her about hearing the horses, she completely freaked. Apparently, she always thought I was spouting poetry when I'd say strange things as a little kid. Ha! I'm about as poetic as a doorknob.

When I told her about "feeling" the horses, she got all weird and started ranting about how she was ruining my life and stunting my emotional and social growth by keeping us out here in the wilderness. She went on and on about how I was "bushed and eccentric." Thanks, Mom.

It took all my powers of persuasion to convince her I was just *pretending* to understand horses, that I was *joking*. She became furious – which was much better than her being upset and worried. Too much worry might make her think she has to leave the Chilcotin, our remote region of British Columbia, to save me from being a social misfit. But I love being a social misfit. I love it here in the wild.

Okay, so now that you know about my psycho psychic ability, back to the mustangs. I *knew* these horses. Willow belonged to their herd. I searched for her thoughts among the pained voices. Was she there? Had she survived, despite what I'd done to her?

I heard Night Hawk, the herd stallion, telling Twilight, the yearling buckskin filly, to not lag behind. Then I focused on the mares and their children: Wind Dancer, a pretty palomino and Twilight's dam, Black Wing, dam of two-year-old Dark Moon; and Snow Crystal, a gray mare so old that she'd long ago turned white. Her latest – and

probably last – foal, a blue roan colt named Ice, ran at her side. My mind went back through the horses, but I hadn't missed anyone. Willow wasn't there.

I blinked back tears. So she had died after all. The accident must have left her too weak to survive this brutal winter.

I got out of bed, pulling my quilt with me and wrapping it around my shoulders for warmth as I hurried to the window on my side of the room. Outside the window was a fairytale land, everything frosted with untouched snow and the moonlight so bright that you knew that if light could sing it would sound like a distant flute's high melody. No moon dogs though, those weird bright patches that appear on each side of the moon whenever ice crystals linger in the air. I was glad not to see them, because they usually mean the coming of worse weather.

But moon dogs or no, I could see it was harsh cold out there. The sky was empty of clouds and the snow seemed strewn with diamonds. The tree branches sparkled. Perfect stillness reigned. It looked exactly as it had for the last two weeks. My forehead touched the window and I jerked back when the glass burned frigid against my skin.

The mustangs were right – it was horribly cold out there, the type of weather that cracked trees and killed wild animals. And they were obviously past the point of being able to fend for themselves. They needed food and shelter.

I couldn't just stay inside where it was warm and let them pass by without doing something. I had to help them.

I put on my warmest clothes and then pulled my second warmest out of my drawers. Mom moved in her bed, disturbed by my noise, even though I hadn't relit the lamp.

Toenails clicked as Loonie walked across the front room and into the bedroom. I knelt down to pet her. She knows she's not allowed away from the door on the super-cold nights that Mom lets her inside, but then again, it's not every night one of your people gets up and puts on masses of clothing.

"Evy?" The toenail clicks must have awakened Mom.

"Yeah?"

"What are you doing?"

I couldn't tell her I *sensed* the mustangs. "There's something moving out there. I think it's the wild horses."

Mom sat upright, then jerked her blankets up to cover her shoulders. "You're not going out there."

"They need help, Mom. I'm going to put some hay in the meadow. It's been so cold and if they've come this close to the house, they're probably starving." I pulled my second warmest shirt on over my warmest.

Mom swung her legs from under her covers. "I'll

come too," she said, then gasped when her feet touched the freezing floor.

"You don't have to. I'll be alright."

I could feel the look she gave me in the dark. "It's too dangerous for you to be outside alone in this weather."

She was right, of course. When exposed skin can freeze in less than a minute, it's dangerous being anywhere outside.

Mom lit the lantern and quickly we bundled up in clothes, hats, coats, scarves, mittens, and boots. I whispered to Loonie through my scarf to stay inside, then opened the door. A frigid wall of air shoved its way into the cabin, making me shiver beneath my layers.

"Hurry," Mom said behind me.

I stood to the side to let her past. I wore way too many clothes to actually hurry. Mom waddled past me and through the door, and I couldn't help but laugh. She turned to look at me following her, then started to giggle. I must be waddling too.

What's wrong? Rusty's question popped into my head. He must have heard us shut the door.

The mustangs are near. They are hungry.

Give food to them?

Yes, will feed them.

Rusty's approval warmed my mind.

"Evy… Evy?"

"Sorry, I… what'd you say?"

I could see Mom shaking her swathed head even in the shadow of the porch. "What goes on in that head of yours when you zone out?"

"Nothing." Then I realized what I'd said. "I mean lots of things. Too many things to talk about."

"I think that's a little closer to the truth." Mom motioned to me to go first.

I stepped off the porch and stomped through the snow to the barn with Mom close behind.

There was a sudden brush of disquiet in the air. Had the mustangs somehow sensed us, even though they weren't close enough to hear our quiet voices?

"We shouldn't talk out loud any more," I whispered. "If the mustangs hear us, they'll take off."

"So you really saw them?" Mom whispered back. The snow crunched underfoot as we walked.

I hate direct questions like that. "I saw shadows in the trees," I said evasively.

"And you could tell they were horses?"

"Yeah. By the way they moved." Of course, I hadn't seen a thing and I hated lying, especially to my mom, but I really didn't have any choice.

"Could you tell how many?"

"Seven, I think." I cringed saying the number aloud. If not for me, there would have been eight.

"Let's put out four bales."

I pulled the barn door open with a heavily gloved hand. The interior was pitch black. Mom and I slipped inside, then Mom shut the door and clicked on the flashlight she'd had the forethought to bring. Rusty, my gray gelding, and Cocoa, Mom's chocolate brown mare, put their heads over their stall doors to watch us. Cocoa whinnied a greeting.

"I'll throw the hay down," I said, a little louder now that the barn door was closed.

Mom handed the flashlight to me. "Be careful climbing the ladder. Your mittens might slip on the wooden rungs."

I nodded and put the end of the flashlight in my teeth to light my way up the ladder. Down below, Mom went to the woodstove at the far end of the barn. A moment later, I heard her open the stove door and throw in some more wood. The barn was drafty, but the stove helped to keep Rusty, Cocoa, and the two barn cats just a little warmer on these screaming cold nights.

In the loft, Socrates and Plato, the two cats, bundled together for warmth. The flashlight's beam caught them on a hay bale near the top of the ladder, looking like a furry round cushion with two heads. Each black cat had one blue eye and one green eye, but on opposite sides of their little faces, so they looked like mirror images of each other. I knelt down to give them a little snuggle and to warm the exposed skin around my eyes at the same time. Socrates mewed when I pulled away and stretched one paw out from the pillow they made together.

"Go back to sleep, guys."

Socrates must have felt the cold because he whipped his leg back inside, then both brothers put their heads down and closed their jewel eyes.

Cocoa nickered again when I threw the third bale down and I heard Mom shushing her, then I chucked the fourth bale over the edge and started down the ladder.

A sound resonates in the dark. The wind? Loose snow falling from a branch? Or soft fur rubbing a tree trunk? I strain my every sense. Is it nothing? Or a predator?

My hand slipped on the ladder rung and back in the barn, I gasped.

"Evy, you're doing it again. The zoning thing." Mom's voice wasn't amused this time.

"I… It's… It's nothing – just a little dizzy. That's all." I felt Mom's hand on my ankle.

I high-step toward the noise. Tree trunks whip past me in the darkness.

"Just take it slow and easy. One step down at a time, okay?" Mom's voice pulled me back.

"Okay." I stepped down and she guided my foot to the next rung.

Air rushes in and out of my lungs as I inhale the sharp air. My muscles thrum with energy, and I ache to pummel any creature that threatens my herd.

I moved one hand to a lower rung.

"Hold on tight," Mom said. "Tighter than that."

I concentrated on strengthening my grip.

I snort into the darkness. Whatever is there – if anything – isn't coming out. I look back and catch Snow Crystal's eye. She will lead the others to safety if there is danger. But this time we may not need to run.

My next step down was firmer, and by the time I reached the bottom, I felt almost normal again. Adrenalin from my reaction to Night Hawk's strong emotions still jittered in my veins, making me shaky, but at least I was breathing normally.

"Are you okay, honey?" Mom drew me into her arms. "What happened?"

I shifted in her embrace, uncomfortable. "I'm not a little kid anymore, Mom. I just felt dizzy, that's all."

She pulled back. "It's these late nights. From now on, no reading after ten."

"Mo-om." Okay, so I sounded just a bit whiney.

"No buts." Her voice was firm. "How late were you up tonight?"

I couldn't tell her I still hadn't gone to sleep. Then she'd think she was right. "After midnight," I said, and it wasn't a lie. Not really.

"From now on, ten o'clock," she repeated. "Now let's get this hay out there so you can get some rest."

I scowled, but she didn't see. She was already hauling a bale toward the door. I grabbed the strings of a second one and dragged it after her.

"We can take them on the toboggan," she said, once the hay was outside the barn. We loaded the four bales on the toboggan, two piled on top of two, and then I walked beside them to hold them steady as she pulled them along. It was tough going as we floundered through the snow, but at least the crust held the toboggan and hay – and compared to the emotions that had been raging through my mind and body just minutes ago, pulling four bales of hay on a thin toboggan through two feet of snow was a piece of cake.

My horse-radar could feel the mustangs settling, relaxing, spreading out, and finally, totally unaware of what they'd eventually find in the meadow by our cabin, they continued to meander in our direction. Their impressions floated toward me: the delight of finding a full mouthful; a tree snapping in the cold and Night Hawk investigating; the two youngest horses forlornly following their dams, hungry and tired, tired, tired. Starvation gnawed at all their bellies like trapped rats clawing their way to freedom.

Finally, we reached the middle of the meadow. I let the bales tip over and then, after Mom cut the strings, I gathered baling twine, shoved it in my pocket, and we both scattered the loose hay around on the sparkling snow.

We started back to the barn, the toboggan skimming over the snow behind us, as light as air. "I hope they find it. It's such a waste if they don't," whispered Mom.

"Me too." I glanced in the direction I felt the horses to see nothing but dark forest. "But even if they don't, something will eat it," I said, deciding to have a bit of fun. "Like moose. Maybe a whole bunch of them will come. That would be cool."

Mom stopped and looked fearfully back at the hay, probably wondering how hard it would be to gather up and carry back to the barn.

"I'm just teasing," I admitted. "The mustangs will have it all gone before the moose know it's there."

"I hope so," said Mom. She was scared of moose, and for good reason. One day last winter, she'd gone out to spend some time with Cocoa. She was walking along, daydreaming about her current painting, when she almost bumped into a massive bull moose hanging out by the barn, looking for food. He chased her back to the house, even fitting under the low roof on our tiny porch, and stomped and snorted for about half an hour. Finally, he became so irritated by Loonie's barking that he left. Loonie might be old, missing some teeth and almost blind, but she can still bark from under the porch. Anyway, since then, Mom has had a very healthy respect for moose.

Back at the barn, we leaned the toboggan against the wall, double-checked that Rusty and Cocoa were still doing fine, shoved one more piece of wood into their stove, and hurried back to the house. The cold had been sifting through my clothes for a while, despite all my layers, and I was *so* glad to get back inside the house. It was like entering an oven. And I'd been cold earlier, just going into the bedroom. Like so many things, cold is relative, I guess.

"It's going to be a while until they find it, isn't it?" asked Mom, as she stared out the big front window at the chaotic lumps of hay darkening the meadow.

"Probably."

Mom yawned. "I'm off to bed then. I want to get Icicles finished tomorrow." Mom names her paintings. "You too," she added. "You need to be awake to do your schoolwork."

"But what if I miss them?"

"The important thing is that they get their food, not that you see them."

"But Mom."

"You can get up early," she said in a tone that told me all discussion was over. I'm only allowed a tiny bit of whining before she shuts me down. She's so completely unreasonable sometimes.

Mom wasted no time getting back to bed and I had no choice but to follow her into the bedroom. But getting up early was no solution. Even if the mustangs didn't arrive for an hour or two, they'd be long gone before dawn.

I crawled beneath my covers on my side of the room, acting both stiff with protest and mournfully silent at the same time, but Mom didn't even notice. She just burrowed into her covers and shut her eyes, leaving me to stare at the dark ceiling.

There was no way I'd be able to sleep tonight, especially since I could feel the mustangs in their wanderings. Their hurting legs, empty bellies, and biting chills shivered through my body, making me feel sick and alone and painfully aware. As soon as Mom's breath became slow and steady, I threw my top quilt around my shoulders and slipped from the room.

The wood stove in the living room glowed a soft orange around the metal door. It was a homemade stove and not airtight, and yet the vague light it made was almost lost to the moonlight streaming in the front window. Quickly and quietly, I stoked up the fire and closed the stove door again, then went to the window and curled up in my favorite reading chair to wait in comfort. Loonie settled on the floor near me.

Snow Crystal was the first to notice the smell of the hay. Astonishment coursed through her body and mind. Then came bubbly hope. Maybe there *would* be food for her suffering foal. Maybe they *would* survive.

Black Wing smelled it next. She stopped and held her head high, inhaling deeply, again and again. The aromas taunted her, teased her senses. I felt her realize it wasn't a dream and move forward.

One by one, the others became aware of the feast that awaited them. Dark Moon, the two-year-old colt, forgot his raw legs. Delight sparked through Twilight and Ice like electricity, energizing every movement.

The only one who didn't seem thrilled was Night Hawk. Suspicion crowded out any pleasure he might have felt as he trotted to the front of the herd. He breathed deep, then stalked forward, every sense on alert. The other mustangs followed him eagerly, hungrily, the youngsters barely able to control their impulse to race to the food.

I held perfectly still as Night Hawk stepped out of the forest. The moonlight played over his thin, furry form as he glared at the hay darkening the open space. He looked back at his herd, at the hay again, and finally at the cabin. I held my breath. Chances were low that he could see me from this distance and on the other side of the glass, but I didn't want to risk anything.

Loonie saw movement and whined. I shushed her, then added, "Good girl. Now, stay." Now was not the time for the dog to bark at the intruder. Even if she barked from inside the cabin, he'd hear her for sure.

Night Hawk's trepidation coursed through me as he stared at the cabin, and after what seemed hours, he looked away. He was satisfied that the dark building was no threat, at least for now. His mind turned back to the hay itself. Was this offering a trap? Why did this food lie here, unclaimed?

Safe. The thought popped out of my head before I could stop it and Night Hawk's head shot even higher. Had he heard me? He must have! Did he recognize my voice as belonging to Willow's killer?

"Please don't panic. Please don't go," I whispered, keeping a tight lid on my thoughts. "I'm sorry. I'm sorry."

But Night Hawk spun around and headed back to the trees at a high trot. Within seconds, he was out of sight. The herd's fear jittered through me when he burst upon them and herded them away. Snow Crystal took the lead and galloped through the trees like a silver arrow. The others raced behind her, their alarm becoming quieter and quieter and quieter… until they moved beyond my range of hearing.

Gone.

Scared? Rusty asked from the barn. He'd heard them gallop away.

Yes. I didn't say anything more because I couldn't. And besides, what was there to say? I felt beyond terrible. First, I'd taken Willow from them and now my carelessness was keeping them away from the food they desperately needed. I was nothing but disaster for this herd. Starving, in pain, and freezing cold, they'd run from the one gift I could give them, the one thing that could save them: nourishment.

It was a long time before I went to bed and even longer before I fell asleep. All I could do was stare through the window at that empty meadow as the moon arched slowly across the sky, and wish them back. But they didn't come. And no matter how long I waited, I knew they wouldn't.

"You're so slow today," Kestrel complained. "I'm going to freeze to death before you get Rusty's saddle on."

I grimaced up at her. Isn't your best friend supposed to be supportive and sympathetic? I'd already told her I couldn't sleep last night. But to be fair, she'd already been out in the cold for over an hour. She and her dad, Seth, rode over to make sure that Mom and I were okay in the harsh weather and now her dad was inside the house, having coffee with my mom. Kestrel would've loved to have stayed inside and soaked in some warmth too, but I had other plans for us. She didn't know it yet but now that I had someone to search with me, we were going to find the mustangs.

"It's positively balmy today," I said, countering her complaint. "You should have been out last night." Maybe she'd take my hint and realize I had good reasons for being slower than normal. And besides, I was right. It was a lot warmer than last night – only 30 degrees below zero instead of more than 40 degrees.

"You went out last night?"

"Yeah, for a little while." I finished tightening Rusty's cinch, then moved to his head with the bridle.

"Why?" When I didn't answer, she added, "What happened? Is it a secret? Does Laticia know?"

"Mom knows some of it."

"Come on, Evy, tell me. Laticia and Dad won't hear us. They're in the cabin."

"Let's get away from here first." Rusty, Kestrel, and Twitchy, Kestrel's bay mare, followed me outside the barn, then Rusty stood resolutely as I swung aboard. He didn't even hump his back, though I knew he was cold too. My heels touched his side and we headed out at a brisk walk. Twitchy stepped out behind him, her hooves landing in the same spots as he broke trail away from the cabin.

"So are you going to tell me what happened or not?" Kestrel asked as soon as we were in the trees, out of sight of the cabin.

"What makes you think anything happened?" I asked in an innocent voice, just to bug her a bit.

"Come on, Evy."

I reached down to pat Rusty's gray shoulder, then pushed his black mane to the left side of his neck. We started to round the small ice-covered lake behind our house. A whiskey jack burst out of the willows that lined the lake, and flapped into the trees.

"Evy!"

I turned Rusty to face her and Twitchy, and smiled. "Okay, okay. Sorry. You won't be mad anymore when you hear this…" I paused for dramatic flair. "The mustangs came to visit last night."

"The mustangs! They came close to your house? You saw them?"

"The stallion came into the meadow while his herd waited in the trees. Mom and I put out some hay. It was Night Hawk and his band."

"That's the big bay with the four mares, isn't it?"

"Three. Only three now."

"Which one's missing?"

"The sorrel mare, the young one with the jagged star on her forehead."

"So you did see them? They *all* came into the meadow?" She sounded confused.

"Uh, yeah," I quickly amended. "But then they must have seen me watching, because they ran away." I looked down at Rusty and his dark eyes caught mine. Only he knew of my terrible guilt. Why had I opened up my big stupid head?

"So they didn't get any hay." A statement rather than a question.

"No."

"It wasn't your fault, Evy. Don't feel bad. They were probably super nervous because of the cabin. A bird might have startled them, or a snapping tree."

"Maybe." Either that or they recognized the voice of a mustang murderer and were keeping as far from me as possible.

The horses were puffing now, especially Rusty. It was hard work breaking trail through knee-deep snow.

"So I'm guessing we're looking for them?" asked Kestrel.

"Yeah. I want to see how they're doing in the daylight. Maybe they aren't as skinny as I thought. It was pretty

dark." Of course, I already knew they were starving. What I really wanted to know was if they were still nearby.

"The poor things. Even the baby?"

"Yeah. They, I mean, *I* call him Ice." A small smile found my face beneath my multiple scarves. Talking about the young horses always made me feel better.

"That's a great name. What does he look like?"

"Completely adorable. He's a cool blue roan color. And remember that buckskin filly from last year?"

"Yeah?"

"She's sooo pretty."

"And the black colt?"

"He's a lot bigger than last summer."

"So he's still there? That's kind of weird, isn't it? I mean, he has to be almost three years old."

"Maybe Night Hawk is waiting to make him leave the herd in the spring, so he's sure to survive on his own. It's been an awful winter."

I pulled Rusty to a quick halt. The mustangs' tracks stretched out before us in a confused jumble of sprayed snow and hoof prints. Obviously, they hadn't slowed for ages after galloping away from the cabin last night. My remorse swelled into monster guilt. Because of me, they'd expended energy they couldn't afford to use. I reined Rusty to follow them.

"I hope they didn't go far," said Kestrel. "Dad will want to head home soon."

"Do you think you'll be able to stay over for a couple days?" I asked, looking back. "I know it's not your usual visit, but maybe your dad will say yes."

A grin broke across Kestrel's face and she patted her saddlebags. "I hoped you'd ask. Dad made me promise I wouldn't say anything unless I was invited, but I have clothes and my schoolwork here."

"Awesome!" Having to stay inside the cabin wouldn't be nearly as difficult with Kestrel visiting. We could play games, talk, do some painting with Mom... Even homework might be fun if we did it together. Joking!

Ow. My leg wrenches as Black Wing shoves me out of the way, beating me to the small mouthful of grass I'd just uncovered from the snow. I whinny a weak rebuke, but sidestep fearfully when Black Wing lays her ears back at me.

I gulp down the grass clump greedily. Heaven in my mouth.

I fought to get over Twilight's dismay and hurt – and to get over Black Wing's intense pleasure as she chewed the mouthful – as I stopped Rusty. If I still felt horse emotions when I was a hundred, I'd still never get used to sensing the same scene from different horses' points of view.

"Did you hear that?" I asked, pretending I'd heard something so I could collect myself.

"No. What was it?" Kestrel guided Twitchy to stand beside me.

I toss my head and turn in an uneasy circle. Where is my dam? She needs to punish Black Wing for stealing my food.

But I knew, because I could sense Wind Dancer too, that Twilight's dam probably wouldn't do anything to Black Wing. Black Wing was the dominant mare of the two.

"Listen," I urged again, even though Kestrel would

never hear them with her ears. They were too far away for that.

She shut her eyes and strained to hear.

Rusty shifted beneath me and Twitchy snorted softly. I heard the reins rub against her mane as Kestrel tightened them. I breathed in sharply as I felt the mustang's location. They were to our right, just half a mile …

An explosion of panic burst through me!

They sensed me? But how could they? We were so far away…

I gripped the saddle horn to stop from falling off Rusty's back, as my mind careened into a wild run.

"What's wrong? Evy? Evy!"

The trees are a blur. Burning pain flares in my shins as I break through the crusted snow.

"Evy, it's not funny. Stop it. What's wrong with you?"

Adrenaline still flooded my body, but Kestrel's voice was almost as frightened as the mustangs and it intruded into their panic.

"Nothing… I'm fine," I managed to croak as the mustangs slowed to a canter, and then a trot. Snow Crystal thought it was a false alarm.

Night Hawk snorted high and loud – was that a shadow moving between the distant trees? The mares didn't seem to think so, but he wasn't convinced. He threw his head back, testing the air, and then trotted a few paces back the way they'd come. Whatever was there, he would pummel it for frightening his herd.

"We should get back. You don't look too good." Kestrel still sounded frightened.

"I'm okay. Just dizzy, that's all," I said, using the same line I used with Mom.

I start my eternal search for grass again. The frozen edge of snow is like a knife's blade on my raw front legs, but still I paw. One by one the others follow my example, and soon Night Hawk returns.

I finally breathe easier.

"We should get back anyway," Kestrel insisted and huddled deeper into her coat. "I need to make sure Laticia's okay with me staying before Dad wants to go home."

"Don't worry. Mom loves it when you stay over. She won't have to stop work to take me for walks."

Kestrel laughed, but her face was still white with tension.

"I don't think it was the mustangs I heard anyway. It was probably a bird or something," I said, turning Rusty toward home. Twitchy was quick to follow. As if taking our cue, far away, Snow Crystal decided it was time to move on – and as the lead mare trotted even farther away, with the others close behind her, the connection between us turned to whispers, then murmurs. Then nothing.

"Why don't we come back out in a couple hours," said Kestrel. "We can look some more after we talk to Laticia."

"Only if you want to," I said.

"We should. If they were the mustangs, they might be gone if we wait."

"Yeah," I admitted. Honestly though, I didn't want to keep searching. I'd learned what I'd come to find out:

the mustangs were still in the area. They hadn't run too far from our house – which meant they may not have recognized me as the killer. Major relief!

But I couldn't say anything to Kestrel, because she'd ask me how I knew they were nearby. Plus I'd never told her about Willow. "Let's go faster," I said. "I'm freezing."

We made good time back to the cabin, even though we slowed the horses a few times when we came to hills and whenever they became too hot. We'd just come into the meadow and were heading straight for the barn when my thoughts returned to the mustangs. They'd startled for no reason again today, and it couldn't have been because of Kestrel and me. We were too far away. Which meant either they were getting super sensitive and seeing ghosts – maybe because they were starving – or something was stalking them.

I hated that the last option made the most sense. Various predators were probably hunting them. The tremendous cold would make more than just the mustangs suffer. Other creatures would be hungry and desperate too, and would be doing their best to survive.

And could I blame them? All creatures need food. All creatures want to live. It just really stinks that some animals need meat to survive, and that in order for one animal to live, another has to die. But that's just the way things are. And there was no way I could protect the mustangs, even if they let me try – which of course, they never would.

Over the next two days, Kestrel and I went out to find
the mustangs during the day and waited for them to
return during the night, but there wasn't a whisper of
their presence. Deer, moose, and smaller animals brave
enough to come close to a human dwelling consumed the
hay in the meadow.

The three of us, Mom included, enjoyed watching the
animals in the moonlight as they cavorted around their
newfound wealth. One big bull moose was the boss of the
menagerie, and as the hay dwindled, he sent the others
on their way one by one. The third night, he was the only
one left to search for stray wisps, his silhouette hulking
and magnificent beneath the bright moon.

"We have to find them today," Kestrel said to me
the next morning as we headed out. Seth, her dad, was
coming to get her that afternoon.

But again, there was no sign of them. They seemed to
have vanished, as if they were mythical forest creatures
instead of wild horses. It was weird, walking through those
frozen forests as if we were the only living beings in the
world. Once, I sensed some fear from Twitchy. The bay
mare caught a stray whiff of something, and for a while

walked with her head almost on Rusty's hindquarters, she was so nervous. However, nothing appeared – no threat, no strange noises, no odd scents – and soon she calmed down.

In a way, I wished we hadn't kept searching for them. I felt confident they'd return after sensing them that first day, but as we rode hour after hour through the bush and I heard nothing, I wondered if they were ever coming back. I wondered if they actually *had* recognized me.

Rusty kept telling me they would return, that they were hungry, that they'd come for the hay when they were desperate enough to overcome their fear, but I wasn't as sure.

Both Kestrel and I were awfully happy to get back to the house on that last day. We sat and warmed our hands around cups of hot chocolate while Mom took a rare afternoon break and made us some lunch.

That afternoon, after Seth had arrived and he and Mom were drinking coffee and catching up on the latest gossip, Kestrel and I dragged four new bales to a clean spot in the meadow. When we finished spreading it out, we looked toward the cabin. Mom was watching us from the window, her face grumpy and her arms crossed. Seth stood beside her and I wished some of the amused expression on his face would slide over to hers.

"She looks mad," said Kestrel.

"She's afraid we're going to run out of hay this winter," I explained. "And I bet she's worried about that big bull moose moving in permanently."

"We can bring over some more hay if you run out," offered Kestrel.

That's what people do here; they take care of each other. "Thanks," I said. "But you know how Mom is – Ms. Do-it-ourselves."

Kestrel just laughed.

Too soon, Kestrel and her dad were riding away from the cabin on their way back to their ranch.

"Come over to visit as soon as you can!" Kestrel called just before they rode out of sight down the trail.

"I will," I yelled back and waved.

Then they were gone.

I kept staring after them.

"Go gather up the hay, Evy." Mom's voice was calm – which was the worse possible thing for the mustangs. She wasn't planning to change her mind.

I turned to face her. "Mom, they're coming back. I know it, and they need it. They're starving."

"Then why didn't they come the last three nights? Every other creature within smelling distance came."

"They're scared."

"They had their chance."

"Kestrel said they'd bring some hay over if we run out."

"We're not going to go begging to our neighbors after throwing our hay away."

"But Mom, there are *babies* in the herd, one foal and one yearling. And another is only two and that isn't very old for a horse," I said, playing my last trump card. "*They* didn't have a choice to come eat. *They* had to go where their mothers told them to go."

Too late, I realized what I'd said. For a moment, I saw tears glimmer in her eyes, and then she spun away. She

33

thought I was really talking about us. She thought I was telling her that *I* didn't have a choice when *she* chose to live here, away from the rest of the world. Which, technically, was true; I didn't have a choice. But I wasn't mad about it either.

"Mom –"

"You… you can leave the hay out," she choked and hurried toward the barn.

"Mom, I didn't mean… I… I'm sorry, okay?" When she didn't slow down, I added, "I already fed Cocoa. She's fine."

"I'm just taking her out for a ride."

"But you can't ride alone when it's this cold out," I yelled after her. "Remember?" When she still didn't answer, I added, "You said it yourself. You can't go without me."

Mom slowed, but didn't stop. "I'll just brush her then." I was about to run after her, to explain that I wasn't upset about living here, that I loved our home, that I'd follow her anywhere – and maybe even ask her one of the many questions that had been burning in my mind for years – but she turned at the barn door and said just loud enough for me to hear, "Alone, Evy."

I stared after her, and the biggest mystery of my life loomed up in front of me once again, as impenetrable as ever. Why had we always lived out here, in the middle of nowhere? Why didn't Mom like going into town or getting to know her neighbors? She'd made an exception for Kestrel and her parents, but I knew that was only because of me. She wanted me to have a friend. She wasn't

34

friendly with anyone else, preferring to remain a recluse. Slowly, I turned toward the cabin. The only other person she had anything to do with was Edward, her agent/broker, who came twice a year to pick up her paintings to sell in his fancy Vancouver gallery and to bring us supplies. She refused to even go into town to buy her own supplies.

She was obviously hiding from something or someone and had been for years, ever since I was a baby.

But who was she hiding from?

And just as important, if not more crucial – Why?

Mom didn't come into the house for two hours and when she did, her emotion was locked behind a face as serene as a field of fresh snow. She'd pushed her worry to the back of her mind and her defenses were back in place, big time. She was even humming.

I hate to admit it, but I'd eavesdropped on her and Cocoa, listening to Cocoa's feelings of peace radiate around Mom as the mare tried to comfort her. As Cocoa's emotion gradually lightened, I knew that Mom was feeling better and better.

And now I had to risk upsetting her again. I couldn't push things out of my mind like she could. I still needed her to understand that I wasn't saying what she thought I was saying.

"Mom, I'm really –"

"There's nothing to apologize for, Evy," she said, before the word could be spoken. "I know it's hard, living out here." She took my hands in hers and looked intently into my eyes. "I promise that it'll only be for a few more years."

"But Mom…" I stopped short. She'd never said so much before. "Why only a little longer?"

Her eyes dropped. "I have so much to do today. And so do you, young lady. Have you finished your report on the industrial revolution?"

I grimaced. I *hate* the industrial revolution. Mom turned away, not waiting for me to answer. Obviously, she was trying to escape my question.

"Mom, when I said that about having to live somewhere because your mom makes you, I was talking about the mustangs. Not me."

Mom glanced back at me. "I'm glad."

I followed her into the corner where she does her painting. "You know I love living here. I'll never want to live anywhere else."

A cloud washed over her smooth veneer. "You won't always want to stay here, Evy. You'll want to get out in the world one day."

I shrugged. "Why? What's out there that isn't better here? You obviously didn't like it much. Why else would you be here?"

Mom glanced sharply at me, then looked away. She wasn't going to take the bait.

Finally, I took my courage in hand and said the words that I'd been dying to ask her for absolutely ages. "What happened, Mom? I'm almost thirteen. I'm old enough to hear the truth. Why are we hiding out?"

I held my breath as she stared out the window. I'd never come right out and asked her before, even though it had been like a massive elephant standing between us for

36

years, both of us knowing it was there and edging around it, and never, ever openly speaking of it – until now.

"It affects me too, you know," I added. "I have a right to know."

Mom stared off into the distance for another full minute and at one point I swear she was blinking back tears. When she finally turned to look at me, I knew I'd pushed her too far. Her composure had been restored. Her face was expressionless and in complete control. I'd get nothing from her this time. "I don't know what you're talking about, Evy," she said, her voice so even and mellow it was almost scary. "We're not hiding out. This is just where we live. Maybe I don't get out much, but I'm working on my paintings and helping you with your schoolwork. I don't see anything wrong with that."

And I said the words I knew she expected. "There's nothing wrong with it. I've just been reading too many mystery books, I guess." Even though I wanted to throw something at her. Even though I wanted to storm out the door and run away to Kestrel's house, where at least people acted normal. Where Kestrel's older sisters talked about people they knew, were loud in their laughter and yelled at each other. Where her mom and dad teased each other, and people were always dropping by for coffee, and no one tried to hide away from the world.

"It's just this cold," said Mom. "We're not getting outside as much and it's giving us both cabin fever."

I nodded, mute.

"And now it's time for you to finish your report."

I clenched my teeth as she turned away and squeezed

some oil paint onto her palette. One thing for sure, even writing about the industrial revolution would be a big improvement over talking to my mom.

I stomped to my study desk, flopped open the textbook, and stared down at the words that meant nothing to me.

However, I'd learned one new thing. We'd be leaving our seclusion in a few years. And the more I thought about it, the more I realized this was a very important bit of information. Why a few years? Was she waiting for something? Maybe she did something illegal and was waiting for the police to stop looking for her. Or maybe she was waiting for her paintings to become popular so she could re-enter the world with a lot of money.

Or was she waiting for me to grow up? The thought hit me like a fist. I'd never considered that *I* might be the reason she was hiding out. Maybe she was trying to protect *me* until I grew up and could protect myself. But protect me from what? Did I have enemies?

I looked over at Mom, busy across the room. She was mixing her colors and seemed to be concentrating. But I could see the light from our big front window play across the tight muscles in her face. She was clenching her jaw too. And she wasn't moving fluidly and without thought as she usually did at the easel.

She wasn't fooling anyone. She was shaken by our conversation as well. She'd realized she'd told me too much. What on earth was going on?

Terrible hunger woke me in the middle of the night. I picked up my wind-up flashlight and crept out of bed as quietly as I could, then clicked it on when I entered the front room. Loonie rose from her mat by the door. When I whispered to her to stay, she settled down again gratefully, as if she'd stood only because she thought she should.

In the kitchen area, I cut a big slice of bread and spread it with homemade butter. It wasn't until I'd taken two big bites and still felt as hungry as ever that I realized the gnawing hunger was from the mustangs. Once again, they were coming close enough for me to sense. Rusty had been right. As usual.

Loonie gazed at me with begging eyes as I tiptoed past her to the big chair by the window, so I whispered to her to follow me. She gulped down the bread and butter that I gave her, then settled at my feet as I stared out at the night.

The loose hay was dark on the meadow and the trees surrounding it even darker. The snow lay unmarred beneath a thin covering of fresh snow, and I realized I was holding my breath as I soaked in the diamond's sparkle and glimmering ice crystals that crusted the surface. If only Mom could paint this light, this serenity. She'd be instantly famous.

I smell heaven, and joy surges through my body. It's still there. Dark Moon pushes past me, rushing toward the deliciousness. I run after him – and I'm called back. So is Ice. My hooves drag as I slow, stop, reluctantly obey my dam. Dark Moon keeps on and every one of my muscles aches to follow him, to rush to the food that taunts us. Loudly, forcefully, Night Hawk demands he return to the herd. Dark Moon ignores our leader and, seconds later, Night Hawk plunges past me, teeth bared, racing after Dark Moon. I am so glad I didn't follow!

In the cabin, I sunk further into their sensations. I felt the pain the colt felt when the stallion bit him, the fear when his sire chased him to the back of the group. But worst than this was Dark Moon's realization he was now doomed to be the last to eat. Next time, he'd listen to Night Hawk.

Cautiously, the mustangs stepped forward, all their senses on alert. I kept quiet in my own mind. If I even thought a whisper at them, they'd be gone, and only wisps of scattered snow would remain where they stood.

Night Hawk stopped his herd when they reached the edge of the meadow, and stepped into the open. I could see him now – a dark silhouette moving from the trees, stepping high and carefully through the snow. He paused. Looked about. Continued. When he came to the hay, he stretched out his neck and sniffed the closest morsels.

Finally he turned his head and nickered to the others. They trotted forward in a group, completely trusting their leader to guide them, and dove into the hay. At last, after weeks of being hungry and cold, they could eat freely of this magical gift that the land had given them.

At first, there were a few minor scuffles. Night Hawk chased Dark Moon to the other side of the hay pile, and Black Wing crowded against the buckskin filly. Twilight's dam, Wind Dancer, bit Black Wing on the shoulder to warn her away from her daughter, and then they settled down to eat peacefully side by side.

It was magical to watch them, to feel their contentment and gratitude for their good fortune. The hay disappeared quickly. Four bales don't go far with seven extremely hungry horses and I watched it vanish with a sense of alarm. Soon the hay would be gone and the horses would leave. I didn't want them to go. Not yet. Well, not ever. They were awesome.

Twilight scampered sideways, galloped and bucked in a circle, then stopped to nip Ice on the shoulder. The two reared together, sheer delight in their movements. Their bellies were full, their good spirits restored, all was well – and so it was playtime.

Their joy was my joy and it took all my self-control to not leap about with Loonie. Their lightness affected the other mustangs too, and soon the last hay stalks lay abandoned and forgotten. Even the old mare, Snow Crystal, ran about, leaping and rearing. Their long, tangled manes and tails tossed in the wind they created and their hooves churned up sparkly snow crystals. Clouds of glitter surrounded them, winking and flashing in the light of the full moon, as they ran and jumped and played.

And so they danced as the moon slid down the sky. I

watched them for a timeless forever as they allowed the beauty of their world to overtake them. I can't begin to write how glorious it all was. Words aren't enough. One thing for sure, I'd never wanted to really truly *be* a horse so much in my life.

But as much as I was there with them, I could never fully enter their world. All I could do was sit in my house on a cold night with my old dog at my feet and listen and watch – and even though it made me sad to know I'd be shut out forever, I also felt unbelievably privileged to glimpse even a brief moment of that magic.

When it was over and the mustangs' dark silhouettes blended back into the forest, when the moon illuminated only rough broken snow, I crept back to bed, knowing I'd never be the same after this night, the night of the crystal dances.

For the next week, Mom and I put out hay every night, and every night the mustangs came back. Mom watched with me a couple of the nights, but then she started to be inspired – painting stylized horses in the moonlight – and worked late every night, watching for an hour or so, then going to bed exhausted. I was glad. I love my mom and I even like her most of the time, but I wanted to listen to the mustangs and I couldn't do that when she was there.

At least Mom understood the enchantment of the mustang's midnight visits and stopped caring if I slept late. She even gave me a break on my homework, thinking that the horses were giving me something unique that books never could. In a lot of ways, she's totally awesome.

As the nights passed, I learned that once Twilight and Ice had eaten their fill, they liked to race a specific course – always the same – around the herd. Not just a circle, but half oval, half triangle, with lots of spinning and kicking along the way. I learned that Wind Dancer was much older than she appeared and Black Wing much younger. She must have been almost a baby herself when Dark Moon was born. I learned that just before the cold

snap started, Night Hawk had been challenged by a rival stallion and had barely kept his herd. He had injuries that were just starting to heal now because of the food we were giving them. I learned that he was waiting for spring to make Dark Moon leave his family, just as I'd suspected, and that Dark Moon felt both scared about being on his own and eager to become a herd sire.

The only thing I never learned was what happened to Willow. She was in their memories, but apparently they didn't like thinking about her leaving them. I was relieved. I really didn't want to know the details of her death.

Every night, the desire to talk to them grew stronger and stronger. I felt I was getting to know them, and after a while, almost felt like part of their herd, so it seemed natural to talk to them. Again and again, I stuffed down the impulse. Night after night, I congratulated myself for withstanding temptation.

I got used to them being nervous as they came and went through the woods to the meadow, and even when they spooked one night – again at shadows it seemed – I wasn't too unsettled.

Then one night, they didn't come. I sat up well past midnight, waiting and staring out at the meadow and its dark lumps of hay. Even after I went to bed, I listened for what seemed hours. But no matter how long I waited, there was no sign of them.

"What is wrong with you this morning?" Mom asked at breakfast, staring at me over the top of her coffee cup. "You're like a bear that hasn't hibernated long enough."

I scowled down at my oatmeal. I hate it when Mom calls me a bear. At almost thirteen, I should be treated with more respect. Next thing you know, she's going to say I need to go to bed earlier.

"So what are you doing up early this morning anyway?" she asked instead, much to my relief. A kid can only take so much.

"They didn't come last night."

"Oh, that's too bad, sweetie." She took a sip of her coffee. "You knew they'd stop coming sometime though. They are feral animals."

"But the cold snap isn't over yet. They need the hay, so why didn't they come?"

Mom considered this as she stared out the window. The morning light showed the dark circles under her eyes. She'd been working too hard lately.

"I don't know, Evy," she finally said.

"I want to go look for them."

"You can't go out alone, you know that."

"Can you come with me?"

Mom glanced over to her work area. A partially finished painting waited on the easel, one of the adult horses with the two foals playing about her. I'm sure it was Snow Crystal with Twilight and Ice, because the big horse looked blue beneath the roughed-in moon. "I really need to paint. The mustangs have given me so many cool ideas; I don't want to lose them."

"Just for an hour?"

Mom sighed. "An hour? Okay. And this afternoon, not this morning."

"Okay." I agreed quickly, before she changed her mind.

"And you have to work on that report on the industrial revolution for four hours."

"Okay." This was said with much less enthusiasm.

Mom rose to her feet. "Well, we both have tons to do before then, so let's get at it." She carried her coffee cup with her to her work corner.

I meandered back into the bedroom and took my time getting dressed. Then I slowly washed up at the basin on the kitchen cupboard. Unfortunately my trip to the outhouse was quick – and I mean *quick*. It was screaming cold out there. All too soon, I was ready to do some more research for that stupid report. Four hours. I could stand that, couldn't I? And then we'd be off to find the mustangs.

Six hours later, Mom finally left the painting of Snow Crystal and the foals. I looked up at her bleary-eyed with boredom. The stupid report lay unfinished in front of me, and the textbook taunted me with irritating facts that I still had to read, organize, and write in my own words. I hate that saying, *in your own words*. The textbook usually says it best and so immediately the students are at a disadvantage because they're forced to write their reports the *second* best way. It makes no sense.

Mom stretched and looked down at me with something like sympathy and another thing like exasperation in her eyes. "How many weeks is it going to take you to finish this report, Evy?"

"It's almost done," I said, trying my best to sound wounded.

"That's what you said last week." She smiled though – to let me know she wasn't really mad, I guess. "So you want to see the finished product or what?" She'd turned the painting away from me that morning to put on the finishing touches. She's never been able to work with someone behind her, even if they aren't watching what she's doing.

"Yes, I do want."

Mom smiled again.

The painting was amazing. Snow Crystal was perfection, all long flowing mane and tail and elegant lines – much classier than she looked in real life actually – yet it was obvious that was who was portrayed. Mom had somehow shown the basic essence of who Snow Crystal was, her maturity, her elegance, her wisdom. The two young horses were pure joy as they leapt around her. Dark trees ringed the trio, and the horses seemed to sparkle in the silver cloud of snow glitter. Mom actually had managed to catch the magic of the moonlit nights.

"It's… it's… Wow, Mom," I finally said. "What's it called?"

"Ice Dances."

"Can we keep it?"

"I don't know, honey. I'd love to, but we need the money. If Edward can sell it, we should probably let it go."

"But if he can't sell it, maybe he can bring it back on his next visit."

"Maybe," Mom said. "But remember, we have something even better. We saw the real thing."

"Yeah, but this would be a great reminder."

She gave my shoulder a quick squeeze. "I know. So how about some lunch?"

"And then we go for our ride?"

"Sure. It'll be fun. It's been ages since I took Cocoa out. This cold is just so numbing."

"I'm going to miss it, in some ways." If it hadn't been for the cold, the horses would never have come near our house. My gaze shifted from Ice Dances to the uneaten hay in the meadow. Why hadn't they come back?

Was there a chance it was my fault? The last night they'd come, they'd been so relaxed. So trusting. Had I relaxed too much too and let a thought slip out without realizing it? If I had, that would explain their absence. Maybe they'd finally tied me to that day last summer, tied me to Willow's death.

Aargh. I guess since I keep bringing up that horrible day, I should tell what happened.

One word, that's all I'd said. One word too many. On a hot July day, I'd crept up on the mustangs to watch them graze. After an hour or so, I couldn't resist greeting the pretty sorrel mare. She jumped as if a thousand bees had stung her at once – and landed in a jumble of branches from a fallen tree. A thick broken branch impaled her shoulder.

I didn't know what to do. I couldn't think of anything other than returning every chance I could to quietly watch her, silently praying all the while that she'd be okay. The broken stick was there for days, as she bled and limped about. Finally it fell out or was knocked away by another horse. But Willow never recovered. She lost weight, then more weight, and then more weight still. All that fall I watched her, hoping to see an improvement that never came. And then winter came – our harshest winter in a decade – and I didn't see the mustangs for a long time. Not until they came to our meadow and Willow wasn't with them. It didn't take a rocket scientist to know what must've happened to her.

Had I done it again, let some stray thought slip that would lead to a death, maybe this time of a starving foal? Regret and sorrow made my throat thick; I couldn't blame the mustangs for not returning if they heard me. They had every reason to be afraid. Mine was the voice that murdered mustangs.

The cold was intense, but the gorgeous afternoon made up for it. Everything was so bright and clear, it was as if all spring, summer, and fall a veil had covered our eyes, preventing us from seeing the stark, excruciating beauty of the land.

The ice crust on the snow dazzled as the horses crunched through it, happy to be out of the barn and small pasture. Rusty kept trying to spring forward into a trot but I didn't want him to get hot or ahead of Mom and Cocoa, so I kept reining him back. Cocoa's not too speedy and neither is Mom. She likes to sit back with a loose rein and stare at everything while Cocoa chooses where they'll go. It's funny how well suited they are to each other. They're both eccentric and have strong opinions, but their opinions and oddnesses match each other.

In fact, that's how Mom got Cocoa. Kestrel's mom, Elaine, brought Cocoa over one day.

"You need a horse, Laticia," she'd said.

"I don't," Mom disagreed.

"Yes, you do, for transportation, and Cocoa here is perfect for you."

That made Mom raise a skeptical eyebrow, but she had to smile when she heard Elaine's reasoning.

Apparently, Cocoa wasn't a suitable ranch horse because she wasn't interested in chasing cows. She'd be gazing off at the mountains and a calf would run right past her, its tail in the air, and she wouldn't even see it.

"Cocoa's a dreamer; you're an artist; it's perfect," Elaine said as her closing argument.

Mom was still reluctant, but Elaine talked her into a two-week trial. By the end of Day One, Mom was totally devoted and so was Cocoa. There's no way anyone could've separated them. Bright and early on Day Two of the "trial," Mom and I rode over to Seth, Elaine, and Kestrel's to pay for Cocoa.

Rusty and I have a similar bond. I've known him since I was little. I don't actually remember a time when he wasn't there. His thoughts have always been in my head, before I could even understand human speech. We love the same things – riding with Kestrel and Twitchy, exploring, and galloping through the forests and meadows. Most important of all, we trust each other. I know he'll always be there for me and I'll be there for him. And it's nice to know I'm not the kiss of death for all horses.

My mushy recollections were cut short by that now familiar feeling of extreme hunger. I stopped Rusty. Cocoa must have been staring off into space because she bumped into his stalled rump, came to a stop, and snorted.

"The mustangs," I whispered, before Mom could say anything.

"Where?" she whispered back.

I closed my eyes to concentrate better. One of the mustangs was thinking of how bitter the willow twigs tasted, so they must be down by Grass Lake. I pointed to the right. "We should tie the horses up here and see if we can get closer."

Mom nodded. She dismounted and tied Cocoa to a tree, patted her on the shoulder, then turned to me expectantly. I stepped cautiously onto the snow crust and bounced. It held. I hurried toward the lake, bending low. Mom was light enough to run on the snow crust without breaking through too. She followed me, as silent as a shadow.

When we drew nearer, I moved behind a tree and Mom did the same with a neighboring tree. I peered around the trunk but couldn't see the lake yet, so I flitted to another tree and looked again. Again and again, closer and closer, being as quiet as possible – which wasn't as easy as it sounds, by the way – we sneaked closer.

And then I could see the lake through the trunks. The snow on its surface made it look like a meadow and willow sticks jutted all around its edge: a ring of brown around a low snowy field.

Gold flashed and I inhaled sharply, then pulled back behind another nearby tree trunk. Mom looked at me questioningly and I motioned in the direction I'd seen the movement. Slowly, she peered around her tree, then looked back at me. She shrugged.

Maybe it was just an odd colored bird. I leaned out

again, slower than slow, and through the tree trunks I saw a golden back among the willows. Wind Dancer.

The mare raised her head and snorted nervously, as if she sensed she was being watched. A forgotten whip of willow stuck from her mouth.

I pulled back. Wind Dancer's unease rumbled through me. She sensed something was there, even though she had no idea what it was, or even if it was a danger. If we just waited and kept quiet, she might go back to foraging and her nervousness wouldn't affect the others.

I heard a whisper of noise and looked over to see Mom running, furtive and light, toward me. She wanted to see what I saw. Tree trunks must be blocking her view of Wind Dancer.

But this time she wasn't careful enough. The snow broke and she fell. The crunch was soft, but to super-sensitive mustang ears, it screamed that something was running toward them.

Wind Dancer stared bug-eyed in our direction for a split second and then the bushes seemed to explode. The mustangs scattered as they jumped away from the perceived threat, an eruption of black, gold, brown, and white.

Mom gasped, but I hardly heard her. The horses' alarm pummeled me. A tidal wave of fear crashed over me.

Predator! Predator!

The horses raced across the snowbound lake, white powder flying in all directions. Their heads arched high as they stared back. They were expecting something to follow, something to race after them. Surely, such a vague sound wouldn't be enough to cause such panic?

The mustangs stopped in the center of the lake, breathing heavily. Steam rose from their hot bodies and their breath was like smoke as their gaze raked the trees. At least they weren't looking only in our direction now. I held my breath and waited, while Mom huddled, still as a stone, watching them. There was a long aching pause, and then the stallion's head lowered and he sniffed the snow. Twilight meandered toward the willows closest to the herd, Ice close behind her.

Wind Dancer chewed again on the bitter willow stick in her mouth. Abruptly, she lowered her head and spat it out. An image slid into her head: our meadow with hay piled in the center. She was comparing her willow stick lunch to the hay dinners she'd had, and the twigs weren't being judged favorably. If only Snow Crystal, the lead mare, would have such thoughts. Then I could be sure they'd be back, still not having recognized me. I probed a bit at Snow Crystal but she didn't seem to be thinking much of anything – just that she was cold. Night Hawk, Black Wing, and Wind Dancer still felt nervous about the sound of the snow crust breaking. And for some reason, the two-year-old, Dark Moon, was still on edge. I was used to him being the foolhardy one, rushing in when the others stood back. Maybe he *was* ready for his own herd.

Snow Crystal leisurely trotted away from us across the frozen lake and the others fell in behind her, single-file. One by one, they disappeared into the forest on the other side. They'd spurned the willow sticks. Did that mean they were planning to have hay in a few hours? Maybe.

"That was amazing," Mom said into the void the

mustangs left behind, her eyes glowing. "I'm so glad you talked me into coming out."

"There's always cool stuff happening out here, but the mustangs are the coolest." I smiled at my mom, then remembered she couldn't see my mouth beneath my layers of scarves. "We should put out more hay tonight, Mom. They're so close to the house that maybe they'll be back."

"Sure," said Mom without a quibble, rising to her feet and brushing the loose snow from her pants. Maybe I'd successfully made her a mustang fan for good. "But right now, let's get back to the house. I'm freezing."

"Me too."

We hurried back toward the horses, our arms wrapped around ourselves for warmth.

"I'm amazed that you knew they were there, Evy. How could you tell?" I sighed. Of course she would think of the one question I wished she wouldn't.

"What do you mean?" Maybe feigning ignorance would help.

"You know what I mean. You knew they were there before you even saw them."

"I just picked up on Rusty's cues," I said, using one of my prepared excuses. "He told me they were there by acting different."

"I didn't notice him doing anything."

"It's not a big difference. You'd have to be riding him to notice."

We reached the horses, untied them and mounted. They were ready to head home too – eager for their barn, hay, and the bucket of oats that they always got after a ride.

"So what does he do that's different?" Mom asked, being irritatingly persistent.

"He, uh, acts interested. And yet not too interested. He steps a bit higher and perks his ears a bit more."

Mom looked at Rusty's ears. They were pointing forward. Very perky. "He looks interested in something now. Do you think he senses something?"

I laughed. "Yeah, that he'll get oats when he gets home." Humor: a brilliant distraction. Mom even laughed. "So," I added to further distract her, "Any ideas for your next painting?"

"Just a little one."

"About the mustangs running across the lake?"

"Maybe."

That's when I knew she had more than a *little* idea. She never tells me about the paintings that she feels passionate about. I looked over at her. She was staring off into space. Preoccupation with her new painting had kicked in, big time. She wouldn't ask any more uncomfortable questions today.

I've regretted telling her about my "gift" so many times, and if I could go back in time and *not* tell her, I'd do it in a second. But how was I to know that she'd freak out – that she'd never forget the conversation, and that every so often she'd feel the need to search my psyche for strange thoughts?

All I can say is thank goodness for her paintings. And thank goodness times two that I figured out a long time ago that asking her about them was the key to avoiding psychological analysis. Right now she was riding along in another world, dreaming about her new painting, planning it, composing it, choosing her colors. And I was riding along, enjoying the last rays of a gorgeous, if increasingly chilly, afternoon, and hoping, praying, longing that the mustangs would come back that night.

Between heartbeats, the dark form leaps from the darkness! It clamps onto my back leg, rips through flesh and muscle! Teeth grind against bone. I scream and kick but the weight is too much to loosen.

Pure survival instinct shoved me back into my own body and I found myself waking in the chair near the window. I was human, not horse. I wasn't out there in the cold, being torn apart by a monster.

The beast jerks me backwards, away from my herd. Each split second is an eternity as my family mills about in front of me, not sure yet what's happening. I scream again.

I tried to force the searing pain to the back of my mind, but it fought my control. And then, when I succeeded just a bit, all I did was open myself to the emotions of the other mustangs. They watched, frozen for an instant, as the dark form slashed at Twilight. The smell of blood assaulted them. Moonlight shone on stained canine teeth. Then Twilight screamed again and I was back with her, feeling every spasm of terror.

I lurched to the door and despite the pain that radiated through my body, somehow pulled my ski pants and winter coat on overtop of my flannel pajamas.

Poor Twilight! I had to save her!

That's when the rage struck me. Night Hawk's fury. Wind Dancer's ferocious anger.

Loonie whined when I flung the door open and staggered outside. "Stay," I managed before closing the door as quietly as I could in her face.

Rusty? I thought, like a mind-wail.

What wrong? asked Rusty, totally reading my panic.

Twilight is being attacked.

Night Hawk struck and the dark shadow released Twilight. A moment later, Wind Dancer and Night Hawk were chasing the predator with snapping teeth and striking hooves.

Rusty was leaning against his stall door when I entered the barn and limped toward him. The alarm was over, though Wind Dancer and Night Hawk's anger still buzzed through my head and my body radiated with Twilight's pain and fear and shock.

Shaking like crazy, I opened the stall door and tried to jump on Rusty's back. But I couldn't do it. My leg had no strength with Twilight's pain infiltrating muscle and bone. I leaned against his side to catch my breath. If only I could block out the agony. If only I could control it. I was about to try leaping to his back again when I remembered that we had an ancient yearling halter in the tack room and limped off.

When I came out, Rusty was gone. I swung toward the barn door. I'd left it open! Did he leave without me? I stumbled toward the door, the halter and lead rope swinging wildly in my hand.

Rusty!

An image of the woodpile jumped into my head. I emerged from the barn to see him standing beside the chopping block, pawing the ground impatiently. I pulled my weight up onto the block and then onto his back, and he sprang into a fast canter. Within seconds, the cabin was out of sight and he was weaving through the dark trees as if he could see every obstacle. I would have slowed him down, but there was nothing I could do or say to make that happen – I hadn't bridled him – so I just held on, kept low over his back, and prayed that I wouldn't be knocked into the snow. No matter how rough the ride, we wouldn't be going far. I'd heard Twilight's cries clearly and that meant the mustangs weren't far away.

Rusty slowed to a trot and neighed loudly. A snow-muffled flurry of sound came from in front of us. The herd was running away. Two emotions battled in my heart: relief that they weren't going to fight me too and a terrible sadness that they thought humans were the worst predators of all. They would face down whatever had attacked Twilight, but humans? Humans were too dangerous.

Something hopped through the snow ahead, a slight form pitching forward again and again, desperately trying to follow the others. Twilight. The filly left dark snow in her wake where her blood marred the pure surface.

Quickly, Rusty moved between her and the departing herd, forcing her to stop. She stared at us, the whites of her eyes bright even in the moon's shadows. Her horror continued to wash over me in wave after suffocating wave. She was beyond terrified now. To Twilight, we were monsters.

Moving as smoothly and slowly as possible – which wasn't smooth at all – I slid from Rusty's back, the yearling halter and rope clutched in my hand. My caution had no effect on Twilight. She tried to spin away, lost her balance, and sprawled on her side in the snow.

Sheer terror lacerated my heart and pain knifed up my leg, almost blinding me with its intensity. I thought I fell to the snow, but wasn't sure if I actually had or if I was just feeling Twilight's mindless panic as she tried to regain her footing. Any moment she expected me to jump on her and kill her… any moment… if she could just stand… if she could just run… why was this happening… moments to live…

Then, just as I was about to lose myself to her extreme terror, I somehow picked up the massive boulder that was her shock and pain and panic and aloneness, carried it through the back door of my mind, and firmly shut the door.

I took a deep breath and opened my eyes. I *had* fallen. I *had* been thrashing in the snow. No wonder the poor yearling was so terrified. I'd been acting like a total psycho.

Shakily, I climbed to my feet. I still wasn't sure how I'd controlled the effects of Twilight's fear – and now wasn't the time to figure it out – but still I felt elated. There *was* a way to control the impressions that came from the horses! I *could* push them down to a manageable level. Though Twilight's fear still coursed through my veins, it was a pale shadow of what it had been just moments ago. Now I could approach her like a sane being. Now I could be more to her than a mirror image of her own horror.

I put out my hand and began to speak in a soothing voice.

It didn't help. Twilight stared at me, still traumatized beyond restraint, and screamed for her dam. An answering neigh, full of heartbreak, came from the darkness, and a wisp of Wind Dancer's torment touched me. But only a wisp.

Twilight shuddered and her head sank onto the snow. I moved a bit nearer and she didn't move, so I moved nearer still. Never happy, now I worried about her *lack* of panic. In fact, I couldn't feel anything from her. I opened my mind a bit more, searching for her voice. She wasn't there.

"Twilight?"

A surge of fear and then nothing again.

What's wrong with her, Rusty?

An image of Twilight huddled in absolute darkness, breathless and still, entered my thoughts. He was saying that she was hiding in her own mind. She was unable to face the terror that was me.

Relief warmed me, but only for a moment. I'd been so afraid that she'd bled to death – an awful lot of the snow around us was dark with her blood. But shock was just as dangerous, especially in this cold. The only difference was that it wouldn't kill her as fast. Instead of bleeding to death, she'd lie there and freeze. Unless I helped her, she'd soon be dead.

I moved closer. She didn't even flinch, didn't even seem to see me. Closer still – and finally, I was two feet away from her. I knelt down and touched her neck.

She pulled away – a good sign. Maybe she wasn't too far gone.

"Good girl, Twilight," I murmured. "Good girl. Good girl." I stroked her neck. She raised her head and I slipped the yearling halter over her nose. When I grabbed the buckle, she jerked back – but I was stronger than she was and held her head in place until the halter was fastened. I was grateful to get it on her quickly. I'd forgotten gloves and my numb hands were weakening fast.

I gave her a quick caress, which she didn't seem to notice, and stood, shoved one hand in my pocket, and pulled on the lead rope with the other.

"Come on, Twilight. Get up."

The filly floundered in the snow, attempting to rise and escape me, then fell back. Her injured hind leg wasn't strong enough to support her weight. She tried again, desperate, and when she couldn't get to her hooves the second time, she panicked again. She churned the snow, running nowhere, and bleated once, just like a lamb. It was the hardest thing to hear, like she was crying or something.

There was only one way to help her and all I could do was hope that it wouldn't send her over the edge of sanity. I wrapped the lead rope around my waist, grabbed the rope in two hands, and pulled back with all my weight and strength. If she would use the rope to brace herself, she might be able to rise to her hooves.

Thankfully, her natural instinct was to pull away from me, and on her third try she almost got her hooves beneath her – but then she pushed too hard, too soon, and went flying onto her side into a fresh bit of snow.

"Come on, Twilight," I begged, and pulled again to

stop her from thrashing. My hands were quickly losing strength, having no protection from the intense cold. I needed to start switching them back and forth between the rope and my pockets to keep them working – but I couldn't pull hard enough with just one hand.

Talk to her, Rusty suggested. *She does not understand.*

I released the rope and stuck my hands in my pockets, then drew in a deep breath. Rusty was probably right. Quickly, I formulated a picture in my mind that I hoped she'd understand, of a horse using the leverage of the rope to regain its footing.

"Okay, Twilight, let's give it a shot." I tightened the rope – but I couldn't make myself send the image to her. She'd recognize me as Willow's killer and would really panic then, I was sure of it. So instead, I pulled with all my remaining strength.

And miraculously, this time she finally clued in to what I was doing! She pulled back on the lead rope, then methodically, purposefully moved her front legs straight out in front of her, and pushed herself to a sitting position.

"Good girl," I murmured and she glared at me. No kidding. The fear was gone that quick. Now that she knew I wasn't going to kill her, she was just plain mad. And in pain. I tightened the rope once more, then braced myself and hoped I was strong enough to hold her steady. Twilight knew exactly what to do this time. She leaned against the pressure, straightened her front legs, and pulled her back end up – and she was standing on one back leg!

But that's where our teamwork ended. Immediately, she lurched to the side and tried to hobble away.

When I stopped her, she staggered one step back, then stood with her injured leg held high. It wasn't flopping, which seemed a good sign. It may not be broken. Now if only the tendons and muscles weren't seriously damaged. I needed to find out, and in order to do that, I had to get her back to the barn and get Mom's help.

Twilight snorted and again tried to escape. This time her attempt was weaker. I really had to get her back to the barn, and soon.

"You can't go with them. You'll die if I let you go. Whatever attacked you will come back and kill you." I pulled gently on the lead rope but she refused to move.

I pulled again, harder, and she stood wavering, still unwilling to give in. Yet. But I knew she would. Soon she'd be too weak to fight.

As if on cue, her head drooped. I pulled hard on the lead rope again and she hopped toward me. I stepped back, and slowly, she followed. Rusty walked behind her, and as we wound our way through the trees, he bumped her occasionally with his nose to keep her moving.

Thankfully, we didn't have far to walk. I don't think she could have made it much farther than the few hundred yards we had to travel. As she bobbed along, the poor thing grew sadder and sadder and felt increasingly betrayed, alone, dejected. And angry.

I tried to ignore her rage, but couldn't push away her anguish and kept brushing frozen tears from my cheeks. I wished I could save her the emotional pain, but how?

I was the fiend stealing her away from everything she loved: her family and her home, the wilderness. I was the one robbing her of the joys and sorrows of being free and wild and independent. The bad guy, that was me, even more than the one who tried to eat her.

But soon she'd see I was the one who had saved her. Soon, she'd realize the truth. I hoped so anyway. After all, she was going to be with me for a very long time.

Mom ran from the barn when we entered the meadow, Loonie bounding before her. Twilight pulled back when she saw the dog and a spike of her fear jabbed my heart before I was able to block it. Resolutely, I pulled it out and forced it to the back of my mind to join the rest of her emotions.

"Keep Loonie back!" I yelled. Twilight jumped and almost fell again at the sound of my voice.

Mom stopped short and called the dog back to her. Loonie obeyed but sat at Mom's feet and whined. Obviously, she was the one who'd turned me in, probably waking Mom shortly after Rusty and I galloped away from the house.

She and Loonie moved well to the side so I could lead Twilight toward the barn. When we drew even with them, I stopped.

"I'm sorry, Mom," I said before she could say anything. "I had to go help her. I should've told you, I know, but I just… well, I just had to go help her. She was attacked by something. A wolf, maybe."

Mom tightened her lips and didn't say a word. There was nothing I could do to fix it right then and Twilight's wound needed attention, so I kept going. It took ages to get the filly inside the barn. The building was unfamiliar and dark, and the flickering lantern light just freaked her out more. She certainly didn't associate barns and illuminating flames with safety and comfort and home, like Rusty and Cocoa. Yet, eventually, she did step forward, and only I knew how much courage it took for her to make those steps. She was an amazing little horse.

Once inside, I led her toward the one empty stall. Our barn isn't very big, with Rusty and Cocoa's roomy stalls along one side, the center aisle with the stove at the end, and a tiny tack room, a small stall, and an empty chicken house on the other side – our last ancient chicken had passed away last fall. Then there was the loft over it all, holding the hay.

When Twilight reached the stall doorway, she straightened her front legs and leaned back. I didn't dare stop pulling because I knew she'd fall if I did. She was already expert at using the pressure on the lead rope to balance herself.

Rusty bumped her with his nose, but still she refused to enter. Going into that tiny little stall was just too much, and she couldn't force herself to do it – until Mom stepped up behind her and ever so gently patted her on the hindquarters. Twilight leapt forward, almost running me over, and Loonie barked uproariously, a bundle of nerves around this horribly unpredictable creature.

I dropped the lead rope – my hands were far too cold to unbuckle the stiff old halter – and left the stall, quickly shutting the door behind me.

I knelt beside Loonie. "Shhh, girl," I whispered, and gave her a hug. "It's okay." When I stood up, Twilight was huddled into the farthest corner. Her eyes, reflecting the lantern light, glowed like angry stars in her face.

"I'll go melt some water so we can clean her leg." Mom's voice was tight, but at least she was talking now. She wheeled away from me and stomped toward the barn doors. When she left, she almost slammed the door. Almost. Either she wasn't as angry now or she was controlling herself around Twilight so as not to stress the poor mustang further. Maybe if I slept in the barn tonight, Mom would be completely over it by morning.

"Stay, Loonie," I said before scooting up the ladder and throwing down a bale of hay. After breaking it open, I put Rusty in his stall and gave a bit to him and Cocoa. There's nothing so calming as listening to horses eat and I thought it might help Twilight, not only to relax, but to eat something too. She was dreadfully thin, despite the nightly feasts we'd given them. Rusty nickered gratefully to me. Not that he was hungry – he just likes food. A lot.

Twilight shrank back as far as she could when I entered her stall with her hay under my arm. I shut the stall door before Loonie followed me, then shushed her when she whined again. She whined louder, obviously thinking I needed protection from the wild beast. I dropped the hay and stepped back outside the stall, and Loonie crowded up against me, pushing into my leg as I leaned on the stall door. I'd wait until Mom returned before going back inside the stall. Maybe Loonie would feel better with both of her humans in the barn.

"Good girl, Twilight," I murmured over the half door.

She shuffled through the straw to put her hind end toward me. I didn't mind. Her new position offered a great view of her injury and – big relief – I could see it wasn't bleeding anymore. However, it was so covered with thick drying blood that I couldn't tell how much damage had been done. Obviously, it still hurt her a lot too – she still didn't want to put any weight on it.

Why was Mom so slow? How long did it take to melt snow in a pot anyway? While I waited, I stoked up the fire. The filly was shivering and though it wasn't freezing inside the barn, it wasn't very warm either.

The barn door opened as I was walking back to the stall and Mom entered, a bucket in one hand and some rags and my gloves in the other. We met at the stall door.

"Sorry, Mom," I tried again. "I really am."

Her eyes seemed softer. She handed me my gloves. "You could have *died* out there, Evy. And I couldn't have helped you. I didn't know where you were and…" Tears slid down her cheeks – which totally made me cry.

I threw my arms around her ribs. "I'll never do that again. I promise I won't. Okay?" And I wouldn't, because now I could control the horses' thoughts and emotions. I would never be overwhelmed again.

She leaned her head on top of mine. "Are you sure you're okay?" she whispered. "What happened out there?"

I told her about all of it, except the part about sensing the horses of course, as we gathered the salve and bandages from the tack room.

"So how do I help?" she asked, when we stood, ready, at Twilight's stall door.

"We have to throw her down and one of us hold her there while the other cleans the wound and bandages it. It's not going to be fun."

"Which do I do?"

"You treat the wound. You know more about cuts and stuff."

"Okay," agreed Mom.

I pushed the stall door open. It wasn't hard to get Twilight down. She practically threw herself during her attempts to avoid us. As soon as she fell, I knelt beside her and held her down by not letting her raise her head. At first she thrashed a bit, but then Mom threw a blanket over her. Either she felt safer, being all covered up, or the warmth lulled her, because it didn't take long for her to stop fighting. Mom moved to her back end with the bandages, warm water, and salve, and started to swab the wound, quickly and efficiently. Years in the bush had made her a very competent nurse.

I stared down into Twilight's eyes. She was looking up at me, once again with fear. Then she moved her gaze away. She didn't want to even look at me anymore. I was that abhorrent to her.

Mom was finished amazingly quickly. When she climbed to her feet and pulled the blanket from Twilight, I unclipped the lead rope from the halter and slowly released the filly. This time she needed no help at all to stand. The bandage must already be helping with the pain.

"Let's get back to bed," said Mom, putting her arm around my shoulders. "She needs time to get used to her new surroundings and you need some sleep."

"I'll get her some water first."

Mom handed me the bucket with the bloody water in it. "Dump this outside, then scrub it out with snow and take some of Rusty's water. His trough is full."

I nodded. Even though I wanted to stay in the barn, Mom was right. Twilight needed to sort out everything that had happened to her. I could feel her information overload like a massive ball of confusion bouncing around inside her brain.

But I wouldn't be able to sleep. I was going to worry all night that she was going to hate me forever. For some bizarre reason, she blamed me for the attack. Then I'd chased off her family, dragged her into the barn, pinned her down in the hay and let another dreaded human hurt her leg. Since I was the one who'd *saved* her, it didn't seem fair. I had to get her to see the truth somehow. She was my horse now, after all.

And that was another good reason to lie sleepless in bed. Who can sleep after getting a new horse? Especially a beautiful buckskin filly: smart, fun, and full of life. Twilight was a dream come true – if I could only get her to stop hating me!

I was wrong about one thing. I *did* sleep, almost as soon as my head hit the pillow. It wasn't until I heard Mom clanging about in the front room that I opened my eyes. I jumped out of bed and rushed to the front room. Mom was bending over the stove, shoving in wood. I could smell coffee and oil paints. A canvas sat upon her easel, with her new painting of horses running over the snowy lake already roughed in.

She looked up at me and smiled. "Hi, sleepyhead."

"What time is it? How's Twilight?"

"Who?"

"The new filly. I named her Twilight," I said sheepishly.

"She's still standing on three legs, but I took her some more water and she drank it. She ate some of her hay too but hasn't touched the oats."

"I bet she doesn't know that it's food yet," I said, as I rushed back into the bedroom to get dressed. This was unacceptable. Mom bringing my filly water and feeding her. Twilight was going to think she was Mom's horse, not mine. "Did her leg look any different?" I yelled and pulled on long johns, then my pants.

"I couldn't tell. The bandage was still on."

I tugged a warm sweater over my head. "Can you help me with her?"

Mom hesitated before answering. "Why don't you wait until Kestrel gets here. She's coming over today, isn't she?"

"Yeah." I hurried back into the front room and headed for the door.

"Breakfast first," Mom commanded.

I stopped short and scowled. "Do I have to?"

Mom put her hands on her hips.

I stomped to the kitchen area.

"There are fried potatoes in the pan on the stove."

I love fried potatoes. Maybe not seeing Twilight for another ten minutes wouldn't be completely unbearable. My stomach grumbled as I dished up my breakfast – potatoes, onions, and moose jerky bits, all fried up in butter and Mom's special mix of spices. It tastes much better than it sounds, believe me.

"I want you to finish that report on the industrial revolution before Kestrel gets here. You've let it drag on for weeks now."

"Are you kidding me?"

Oops. Wrong thing to say. Mom's eyes flashed. "I'm not kidding you. Get it done, or I'll send Kestrel home right after she warms up."

Okay, so fried potatoes didn't make up for this torture. I was away from my new horse *and* being forced to think about the stupid industrial revolution. I carefully kept my opinion about how unfair Mom was being to myself.

Then I noticed Loonie looking in the window from the front porch. "Why is Loonie outside?"

"It's warming up."

I took another big bite of potatoes.

"If you spent as much energy on that report as you did on avoiding it, you'd have been finished ages ago," Mom observed.

I took another big bite. I simply had to get out of here.

At last Mom got the hint from my silence and moved to her easel. As I shoveled potatoes into my mouth, she stared at her painting, and then slowly, not taking her eyes from the canvas, reached for her paintbrush. She was off to dreamland again. Finally!

When I left the house, Loonie greeted me as if she hadn't seen me for months – you just have to love dogs. And Mom was right. There was a change in the air. It was still cold, but I didn't feel the sting on the skin around my eyes. I sighed through my scarf and tried to cross my gloved fingers. If only the cold snap really was over, the mustangs would be so much better off. They'd easily be able to paw through the softened snow crust to find food, plus they wouldn't need to find as much food to keep up their body heat. Also, if it continued to get warmer, they might even find melted water on the ice to drink, instead of having to eat snow.

Loonie dashed around like a puppy, sending up sprays of white. I couldn't help but laugh out loud. The cold had to be on its way out for good; Loonie only acted this silly when spring was on its way.

Rusty and Cocoa neighed enthusiastic greetings when

I opened the barn door. I grabbed some hay and carried it to Rusty's stall, but then realized that his manger was already half full. Of course, Mom wouldn't feed only Twilight. Still, he looked so eager for new hay that I gave him a thin flake. After returning the hay to the broken bale, I went to Twilight's stall.

The filly was still standing in the far corner, still glaring at me, and still not putting any weight on her back leg. The very tip of her hoof barely rested on the ground, and her entire limb trembled, though the movement was almost imperceptible.

I unlatched the stall and Twilight's fearful anger covered me like a fog. Ever so methodically, I went through the mental motions of picking up her emotions and taking them through the back door of my mind, leaving a crack so I could be a little aware of her feelings. Then I took a deep breath and slid the rest of the way through the stall doorway. Twilight hunched up her back.

"Be still, pretty girl," I whispered. "I'm not going to hurt you. I'm going to make you strong again, if I can."

Her leg had swollen since last night. I reached out for her, thinking that if she let me scratch her shoulder, I could slowly move along her neck, toward her head and halter where I could control her – but she shied away and hobbled to the farthest corner, then swung her hindquarters toward me and pinned her ears. I almost laughed. Like that was going to stop me.

I edged toward her, whispering as I went and keeping to her wounded side. She wouldn't want to kick me with that leg, I reasoned. Her head turned farther to the side as I got closer. And then finally, I was near enough. I double-checked her feelings – a bit more fear than anger right now.

She flinched when I touched her. Gently, I scratched the top of her hindquarters, talking to her all the while. Her hair was thick and fuzzy, kind of like Kestrel's collie's fur, all soft and poofy. After a few minutes, I moved my hand to her back and stepped closer to her head. Scratched and rubbed and scratched again for long minutes.

Finally, she relaxed her ears, then, her head lowered and she sighed. Her bottom lip twitched with enjoyment. I shifted closer to her shoulders and she instantly stiffened, but then realized that a shoulder scratch felt good too – and then a neck scratch, a chest scratch, a chin scratch, and finally behind her ears.

Her eyes, dark in her golden face, appeared even larger than they were because of the black lining around them. She looked like she was wearing mascara, and as if she'd dipped her nose in ebony paint. The edges of her ears were lined in black and her mane was almost blue it was so black. Her tail was black too, and her legs up to the knees and hocks. She even had a dark stripe down her back. But the rest of her was gold. Not just any yellow gold, but a warm, burnished color, as if the sun had marked her.

"You're so pretty, Twilight," I murmured and alarm flared in her expression for a moment. I couldn't help but smile. We were all going to be best friends, she, Rusty, and I. I could just feel it.

With fingers aching from all the scratching, I finally drew away. I'd decided against grabbing her halter, as she wasn't trying to escape me anymore. Now, I'd give her a couple of minutes to eat or drink or move about before starting to work on her other side. Horses are weird that way. They can be totally familiar with something or someone being on one side of them, but then act like you're the scariest thing in the world when you move to their other side. With Twilight being a wild horse, I knew it would probably take almost as long to get her used to me standing on the second side.

I gave her a gentle pat on the rump, then went to the grain bin and measured oats into two buckets. Cocoa and Rusty watched me eagerly, their ears pricked forward.

"Hey, buddy," I said when I put the bucket in Rusty's stall. He shoved his nose in the bucket, not bothering to nicker in reply. His pleasure in taking the first oats into his mouth was a lovely lightness, tap-dancing through my awareness. Cocoa nickered impatiently and struck the stall door.

"Coming."

After the two horses had eaten their oats and received a good grooming, I opened Rusty's door to the outside. He trotted out and snorted loudly, then leapt straight into the air. I followed to watch him run across the pasture, then went to open Cocoa's door. She raced after him, twisting her body into crazy bucks. Snow flew around them both like sea foam.

I tipped my head back. A thin skiff of clouds covered the sky. The blue was white now – so it would be getting warmer still. The mustangs were going to be all right.

Even the creature that had attacked poor Twilight would be better off.

Loonie could sleep outside again and guard the cabin and barn – and unfortunately, she'd keep the mustangs away. But maybe that was okay. If they came again to our meadow, Twilight would sense them, and she didn't need that pull from her old life. She was a domestic horse now.

Another great thing about the warmer weather was that I could go riding without an escort now. I wouldn't have to wait until I could force Mom away from her paintings. I could even ride over to Kestrel's by myself. Rusty and I could go exploring again – this time with Twilight too. The thought made me feel warm all over. I felt outrageously free and happy.

But enough time wasted. Kestrel was going to be here soon, and I wanted to teach Twilight that I wasn't scary before she met yet another beastly human. Also, I eventually wanted to clip the lead rope to her halter and teach her not to be frightened of the rope. It shouldn't take too long as she already had some experience with it – if she remembered anything from last night. She'd been totally spaced out.

I closed the outside doors to the horses' stalls to keep the stove's heat inside the barn, and continued my planning. I wanted to teach Twilight to stand while being groomed. Then, as soon as her leg was better, I'd start the leading lessons. I'd show her to pick up her hooves for me to clean…

So many cool things to do.

"Evy? Are you in here?"

I moved away from Twilight's right side – I'd almost scratched my way to her head again – and slipped out of the stall before answering. Kestrel was petting Plato just inside the door; he purred so loudly, he sounded like a small motor.

"Hey. I thought you'd never get here."

"What are you doing?" Kestrel asked.

I smiled. "Spending time with my new horse. Come see her."

Kestrel rushed to the stall door and Twilight jumped into the far corner of her enclosure again.

Another one, I could hear her thinking. *How many can there be?*

Kestrel inhaled sharply. "Oh, she's so pretty. Laticia said you had a cool surprise, but I never would've guessed. Where did you get her?"

"She's one of the wild ones. Look at her back leg."

Kestrel gasped again, this time not with delight.

"She was attacked in the trees near the meadow last night. The herd came for the hay and something was lying in wait. I think it's been hanging around for a while now, hoping to get one of them." As the words came from my mouth, I knew they were true. That alone explained the mustangs spooking at nothing – or what seemed like nothing. And I realized something else: the attacker probably knew the path the mustangs normally travelled to reach the hay. It could've been waiting for them to pass, which could be why they stopped coming – until they got too hungry again, that is.

"Do you know what it was?"

"A wolf, maybe. I'm not sure. If it is, it's a weak one. It didn't do nearly as much damage as it could have."

Twilight was feeling less fear now, but no less frustration. Her ears flattened against her skull and her resentment was a beast snarling through her mind as she listened to us.

"She's lucky she's not dead. Tell me everything, in detail."

Using the most lavish detail possible, I told Kestrel all that had happened since the last time she'd visited: the mustangs coming every night for while, then getting spooked, probably by the wolf, and Mom and I going out to see if they were still around. Then there was the attack on Twilight, which I said I heard with my ears, and the wild ride on Rusty's back as we raced to the rescue, the gargantuan effort it took to bring Twilight home, and Mom's anger, and well, everything. By the time I was done, Twilight was looking even grumpier, as if my voice was the most annoying thing she'd ever heard.

"All the exciting stuff happens to you," Kestrel

complained, then added with a smile, "Thank goodness. I kind of like sleeping the whole night, warm and safe in my own bed. It would be awful to hear an attack and have to run out into the dark to save someone." She turned appraising eyes on Twilight. "But how amazing that you saved her life."

"Yeah, that makes it worth it," I said, though there was a lot more than that which made my ability to understand horses worthwhile. Last night had been scary, sure, but it had been exhilarating and fantastic too. But I didn't want to make Kestrel feel too bad about missing out.

"She's really pretty, Evy, but do you think she'll heal up enough to be sound?"

"I sure hope so."

"I guess it doesn't matter if she has a permanent limp. As long as it doesn't hurt her and she can still move fast, she'll be okay out there." When I didn't immediately respond, Kestrel knew something was up. "You *are* planning to turn her loose when she's better, aren't you?"

I shrugged. "Maybe," I said, even though I had no intention of letting Twilight go. When that halter went on her head last night, she became mine. "So can you help me check her wound? We'll have to re-bandage too."

"Sure, no problem. Laticia said you needed my help."

I opened the stall door.

"And she said something else too." Kestrel sounded puzzled. "Something about a revolution calling you? What's that about?"

I groaned. I'd forgotten all about the stupid report. "It's homework – homework of the most stupid, boring, waste-of-time kind. I was supposed to have a report done before you got here and I totally forgot."

Kestrel laughed. She understood. She's home schooled too, but a teacher directs her education through the mail. Mom just gives me stuff to learn. "We can work on it together, okay? It'll be fun."

"Uh huh – *fun*. But yeah, I'd love your help." I picked up the lead rope. "I'll go in first and get the rope on her, and then you come in, really slow, okay?"

"Okay.

It didn't take long to get the lead rope hooked to Twilight's halter. Though she was nervous of its snaky appearance, she wasn't really scared of me anymore. I just hoped that not being as scared would translate into being more trusting and calm too, otherwise the next few minutes were going to be unpleasant.

They weren't just unpleasant; they were *extremely* unpleasant. Twilight didn't want us to get near her injury, let alone touch it. Kestrel stood at her head, clinging to the halter with both hands, while my miserable, angry horse rolled her eyes and fought us every way she possibly could.

The second time Kestrel was smacked into the side of the stall and the third time I was kicked – yes, with her injured leg, that's how desperate she was to escape – I knew we had to try something else or we'd never get the wrapping changed. I stepped away from her leg and Kestrel released her tight hold on the halter. Twilight hung her head, tired but unrepentant.

"I don't want to throw her again," I said. "I hate forcing her."

"We might have to," said Kestrel, rubbing her shoulder.

Talk to her, said Rusty.

No. I can't. You know why.

"Let's try one more time," I said.

Kestrel groaned.

Twilight's muscles quivered beneath my hand when I touched her shoulder. She was so tired that this would have to be our last attempt. It was better to throw her than exhaust her when she needed all her energy to heal. "Let's stand her against one side of the stall."

Then listen, said Rusty.

Now listening I could do. As Kestrel positioned Twilight, I opened my mind to the filly's feelings – and realized something. She wasn't objecting to the pain as much as the confinement. She hated having her head held so she couldn't see what I was doing.

"This time don't hold her halter when I try to clean the wound," I said. "Keep the lead rope loose, so she can see me."

Kestrel looked at me like I was crazy. "Are you sure?"

"Yeah. She won't kick me if she can just move away, and she won't push you around either." It made so much sense. Why hadn't we thought of it before?

Kestrel stayed by Twilight's head, but let the lead rope hang loose, and I edged toward the filly's wound, bucket and rags in hand.

Twilight glared at me.

Kestrel raised her eyebrows.

I patted my filly on her rigid back. "Now be good,

Twilight. I just want to help you." She trembled as I slid my hand down her back leg to the top of the bandage. I paused there for a long moment to give her time to accept my touch, then cautiously began unwinding the soiled cloth. Twilight's pain reverberated through my heart as I gently pulled the bandage away – and yet she didn't move. Two tense minutes later, the soiled length lay in the straw, filthy and caked with blood.

"Okay, girl, you did good. Now I just need to wash it. This shouldn't hurt as much." I patted her hindquarters and she flinched.

I wrung the cloth above the wound and let the warm water trickle over it. Twilight's shock, and then reluctant delight at the warmth, coursed through me. At least, she liked this part of her treatment.

As the gobs of blood and other gunk slowly loosened and fell from her wound, revealing it in all its horrible rawness, I felt my throat close off. It looked so gross. There was even some white stuff there – I didn't know what it was, tendon or bone, but I knew it couldn't be good. Neither body part was meant to be exposed. I couldn't even hope for no scar. She was practically guaranteed a white streak down her back leg for the rest of her life.

I gently smeared on the salve, then pulled the clean bandage from my pocket and started to wind it carefully around the wounded leg. We were going to get awfully good at this, Kestrel, Twilight, and I. Seeing the wound in all its ragged glory made me realize that we'd be doing this for a long, long time. Maybe even into the spring.

Finally, I straightened. "Good girl, Twilight," I said. She turned her head as far from me as she could. Obviously, she didn't care if I thought she was good or not.

"She was great. I can't believe it. How did you know that her head being held was the problem?"

"I didn't. I was just desperate to try anything different." I gave Twilight a final pat and Kestrel slipped her halter from her head.

"You should be a horse trainer. Hey, you want to help me with Twitchy? She drags her feet halfway here and then starts to race along, trying to get here faster. What should I do?"

"I don't know." We moved toward the stall door.

"Well, guess, oh genius horse trainer."

"Um, take some oats with you and give them to her halfway? And then don't give her any when you're here. After a while she might get faster at the beginning and slower at the end."

"That's brilliant, Evy." Kestrel actually sounded impressed.

"But of course," I said, haughtily.

Kestrel punched me lightly in the shoulder and Twilight moved farther away from us. "So you want to do your homework now, genius?"

I wrinkled my nose with disgust. "Yuck."

The report didn't take too long, once we sat down and actually concentrated on it. And Kestrel was right. It was even a *little* bit fun to work on together. Part of what made it fun was throwing in some mistakes on purpose to see if Mom would actually read the entire thing. Like saying that part of the labor that children were forced to do back then was writing horrendously boring reports that no one ever read. And that the first printing press newspaper headlines read: "Steam Power Blows."

By the time we were done, the late afternoon sun angled across the snow. Night falls early up here. Four o'clock in the afternoon, and already dusk was upon us. Kestrel and I rushed outside to bring the big horses in and to spend a bit more time with Twilight while Mom made dinner.

As the sun set over the mountains, we let Rusty and Cocoa into their stalls, then roped off the stove so Twitchy couldn't get near it and left her to sleep in the barn aisle. Twilight was taking the stall that Twitchy normally used.

All three of the adult horses dove into their hay and grain with gusto. As I groomed Rusty, I decided to ask Mom if we could convert the old chicken house area to a fourth stall, now that I had two horses.

The chicken venture had been a miserable failure and one I'm sure she didn't want to repeat. It had started out okay, with young hens and lots of eggs. Loonie especially loved our egg period. She got so shiny from all those raw yolks. But then the chickens got older and stopped laying so much, until one day, the old dowagers gave us their last egg. Elaine told my mom that we should butcher them. They'd be tough birds, being so old, but still good for stews, she said.

However, Mom couldn't do it. She couldn't even give the word for Kestrel's mom and dad to do it for us, because she figured that would still make her responsible for their deaths. In her opinion, the birds had spent their youth giving us their eggs, so we'd care for them when they were old. Every single hen died of old age, a precious and respected matron, which was great for the chickens, but not so good for our money situation. Those eggs we got in the early years were awfully expensive when we took into account all the unproductive years we bought chicken food. Anyway, that corner of the barn was totally unused now, and it would make a great stall for Twitchy when she stayed over on the cold nights.

When we brought her grain, Twilight was lying in the corner of her stall, her head resting on some hay she'd pulled from her hayrack.

"She's not stuck down there, is she?" asked Kestrel.

"I hope not."

Twilight answered our question by rising ungracefully to her hooves and backing into a corner, as if she expected us to maul her back leg again. I put her hay back in the rack and topped up her water, then left some grain in a bucket. She still hadn't tasted the oats, but I figured it was just a matter of time.

We leaned on the door for a while and watched her watching us and talked about her future. One scenario included her jumping over the arena fence at the local rodeo to save me from a mad cow and being discovered by a rich and famous show jumper, who offered us massive amounts of money. Of course, when I said I'd never sell Twilight, the famous show jumper had to take both of us to her fancy stables to train, and we went on to become world champions. And there were some other crazy imaginings too.

When night had completely darkened the tiny window behind Twilight, Kestrel and I started back to the house, talking a mile a minute and already making plans for tomorrow. First order of business, of course, was turning my wild filly into a polite domestic horse. I was confident we'd have no trouble, not with time and patience. Twilight was just a little stubborn, that's all. And second, we wanted to make sure that the predator who had attacked Twilight was really and truly gone.

The next day, after the horses had their breakfast and the first chill was out of the air, we rode out looking for the nasty creature that had attacked Twilight. It was more than curiosity that made me want to be sure it was gone. Something about the attack didn't make sense.

For a predator to stalk the same horses long enough to know where to wait along their trails seemed odd. The predators around here usually range far and wide to find prey. They don't usually follow one group around, hoping for an opening because that group knows they're there after a while. The element of surprise, a huge part of any attack, is lost. And to make things more suspicious, this predator hadn't chosen a very good time to go after Twilight. Attacking her when her sire and dam were right there to save her was a major blunder.

So it was a mystery, and Kestrel and I love mysteries. Our first step in solving this one was to go where Twilight was attacked.

The snow was trampled and discolored with old blood, as if someone had sprayed it with rusty brown paint. I could see where Twilight had thrashed in the snow, and where I had, too, before I'd learned how to push her panic and pain to the back of my mind. Embarrassed, I turned my back on the flattened snow and hoped Kestrel wouldn't notice.

"So what are we looking for?" she asked, staring down at the old blood with distaste.

"Tracks? I don't know. Anything that looks interesting."

She looked around at the battered snow, and farther out, the myriad tracks. "Well, there are lots of horse tracks."

I started to scout around. Rusty followed me, his nose almost in my jacket hood, then suddenly he stopped. *Wolf this way,* he said. So he thought it was a wolf too. He snorted and walked to my right, pulling me gently and firmly along with him at the end of his reins.

"What's he doing?" asked Kestrel.

"I don't know," I said, trying to sound surprised. Rusty stopped and sniffed at the snow in a relatively untrampled spot – and there they were. Tracks.

"It's a wolf," I said for Kestrel's benefit, seeing the large canine prints in the rumpled snow. "A big one."

"Wow, cool. Good job, Rusty." Kestrel was already mounting Twitchy. "Let's follow them."

The tracks led onto the snow crust where they were harder to see, but not impossible, and then to a spot nearby where the wolf had waited for the mustangs to pass.

"There's no point in backtracking it," I said. "We need to see where it went, not where it came from."

"I agree," said Kestrel. We rode around the place where Twilight had been attacked until we reached the untouched snow and eventually the wolf's tracks again, arrayed in the skiff of snow over the snow crust. Great spaces stretched between each stride, as if it was running

96

for all it was worth. And alongside it were a horse's tracks. I could just imagine Night Hawk or Wind Dancer racing along beside it, reaching with yellow teeth to bite it as it ran. I hoped the mustang got in a few good ones.

Eventually, the horse tracks stopped where the pursuer gave up and went back to the herd. The wolf tracks kept going. Soon the spaces between its long leaps lessened. Then it was obviously just loping along, in that ground-covering stride that wolves do when they want to cover a lot of country quickly and efficiently, at a pace they can maintain all day and night.

But then the strides grew shorter, and finally, it was trotting, then walking across the crust of the snow. Was there something wrong with it? There was no blood on the snow to mark its passing, but maybe it had been injured internally by Night Hawk or Wind Dancer, or even by Twilight as she struggled to free herself from its savage grip.

We followed the tracks as silently as we could as the morning crawled along. It was hard to keep quiet in the bright, cheery, relatively warm day. Kestrel and I usually only saw each other every couple of weeks in the winter, and there was always lots to talk about. But we could come across the wolf at any time; we needed to be concentrating, not gabbing.

The tracks stopped at the bottom of a dirt and rock ridge. The incline was too steep to hold much snow, but as I searched its surface, I saw scuffs of snow marking the rock here and there. The wolf had climbed the ridge. And on second glance, it didn't look like it would be that hard to follow. There was a narrow trail, or outcroppings at least, to step on, all the way to the top. I signaled to Kestrel that we should climb up and she nodded so we dismounted and tied the horses to tree branches.

"I'll go first," I whispered at the bottom of the incline.

"Don't loosen any rocks to fall on me."

"I'll be careful." But it wasn't as easy as it looked. The "trail" that scooted up the rocky hillside was pitted and uneven and not remotely used to heavy traffic. A wolf would be fine with its weight evenly distributed on four neat paws, but humans with their big flappy feet? That was a different story. I used my hands a lot and, bit by bit, we moved upward.

Halfway up we paused to catch our breath. Maybe it would've been smarter to try to find a way around the bluff. What if the wolf's tracks just continued on at the top? We couldn't leave the horses below and follow on foot. However, we were too close to the top to discuss it now, even in whispers, so I kept going.

At long last, we reached the top. Before looking over the edge, I waited until Kestrel was beside me – then together we slowly raised our heads over the lip of the ridge. The land dropped on the other side. We lifted higher. There were the tracks, leading down a gentle slope. Down, down, down – straight to the wolves. Two scrawny puppies sprawled in the sun in front of their den, panting in their sunbath.

They were both black, with bones jutting beneath their rough, unhealthy coats. How long since they'd had a good meal? Before the cold snap that started weeks ago? I felt tears well in my eyes. I certainly didn't like what the adult wolf had done to Twilight, but it had just been trying to save its babies, probably born late in the season. The pups needed food desperately and, sadly, the adult wolf was probably just as weak as these two. No wonder it didn't range far and wide to find food. No wonder it had simply tagged along after the mustangs whenever they were nearby, until it knew their trails, and then waited for them to pass.

A sudden thought struck me and I quickly glanced around, then looked down the cliffside to Rusty and Twitchy below. Where was the big wolf now? Dead from starvation? Or hunting? Hopefully, it was alive, but not nearby and planning on almost-teenaged girl or domestic horse for lunch. I motioned to Kestrel to go back down. Carefully, we retraced our steps, and at the bottom returned to the horses.

"We need to get them some food," said Kestrel, as if she'd read my mind.

"We can give them some moose jerky. We don't have lots left though. Mom might get mad."

"We have lots of beef at home. I'll bring you some next time I come."

I grimaced. "You know Mom. She won't accept charity."

"It's not charity. It's just repaying what *I* borrowed from you to give to the wolves. Right?"

"Right." I grinned. Kestrel can be pretty sneaky.

We trotted home, put Twitchy and Rusty in the barn to have an oat snack and a short rest before we headed out again, and were just edging around the cabin to "borrow" the jerky when the smokehouse door opened and Mom stepped out.

"There you are," she said, totally unsuspecting. "Come in and have some lunch. I made cookies to celebrate Kestrel's visit. They're almost ready to take out of the oven."

I must admit that we weren't too broken hearted about going inside to eat, though I felt a bit guilty about the starving wolves as I ate my cookies. But their trials would soon be over – as long as the adult wolf was still alive and hunting. The warmer weather would help it catch food, because the small prey wouldn't be hiding away from the cold, and in the meantime, the jerky would give the pups a nutritional boost.

It was late afternoon before we could get away without creating suspicion. We got the horses ready quickly, and then I ran to collect a big bag of jerky while Kestrel stood watch.

Still, despite our hurry, night was riding our heels by the time we got all the way back to the wolf's ridge. I put the bag over my shoulder as I started to climb, Kestrel right behind me. At first it was easy making our way up the slope again, but as dusk descended, it became harder and harder. I wasn't sure how on earth we were going to get down again, but now wasn't the time to worry about that.

At last we reached the top. Just like before, we peered over the hill. There was the den, but there were no wolves in sight. They must be inside – or possibly lurking about in the half-dark. A shiver jittered down my spine. Because they were black, they might be in the shadows near us and we wouldn't see a thing.

Kestrel and I kept our eyes on the opening of their den

as we took chunk after chunk of meat and threw it toward the black hole. Then we started back down.

Climbing down was worse than I imagined it would be – and it didn't help that halfway down, we heard the wolves up above. The two pups were fighting over the food. Then a loud roar drowned them out – the big one, trying to get them to stop, I guessed. However, despite its parental intentions, it sounded terrifying. My heart quickened, I moved a little too quickly, a little too jerkily – and lost my balance. I tipped backward, wildly grabbing for anything that could save me, and my hand closed on a loose rock!

If Kestrel hadn't grabbed me, I would have fallen. As it was, the rock went spinning into space and, moments later we heard it hitting tree branches. The wolves stopped their squabbling to listen. All sound became as frozen as the land.

Then we heard them again, fighting over the food. Relief swamped my body.

Kestrel stopped moving along the narrow rocky trail. I thought she just needed another moment to steady her nerves – I needed it anyway – but then she grabbed my shoulder. The whites of her eyes shone in the half-light as she pointed upward, and my breath caught in my throat as I looked up.

A massive black wolf stared down on us. Its dark form was etched against the night sky and I could see the glint of the last light on its teeth. It looked to the right of us and growled, and the low rumble stole the final bit of air in my lungs.

Then quick as thought, it was gone. The pups immediately fell silent.

Kestrel and I strained to hear a sound, any sound. And I did. One of the horses stamping the snow below us – and to the right.

Everything became clear. It had seen us, no doubt, stuck on the ridge. And it had seen the horses tied up. This wolf was no dummy. It wasn't going to gulp down scraps when captured prey waited patiently below, prey that could feed its pups for a couple of weeks. It was on its way to bring down one of the horses.

Wolf coming! I mind-shouted to Rusty.

I could feel fear surge through him, and then Twitchy reacted to his panic by throwing herself back against her reins. The branch bent back, but the reins were thick leather and didn't break. She strained for a moment, then jumped forward again.

"Come on, Evy," Kestrel said. "Come on!"

I snapped my thoughts away from the horses. We tried to rush along the slope but it was too dangerous to go very fast, and because of the blood pounding in my head and every cell in my body screaming at me to hurry, hurry, hurry, we seemed even slower than we were.

Then Rusty sensed the wolf. It must have run around the other side of their hidden home, then circled around behind the horses. I could feel its presence in Rusty's mind, a terrifying shadow monster slinking through the tree trunks toward them.

"It's down there," I gasped to Kestrel – but my best friend was gone!

She'd jumped!

I looked down. The snow was only eight feet or so below us, and Kestrel was already picking herself up and running toward her horse. Taking a deep breath, I leapt from the cliff.

My knee hit a rock beneath the snow and for a moment, all I could do was lie there in a bath of pain. But then Rusty's fear careened into my mind. Somehow I scrambled up and staggered toward him.

"Hurry, Evy!" Kestrel shouted. She had already untied Twitchy and was moving to Rusty's head now. And then the three of them were running toward me, one set of reins clasped in each of Kestrel's hands. "Are you okay?"

"Yeah," I croaked, even though the pain radiating from my knee up into my hip and side made my whole body quiver. I felt weaker than a mouse. I leaned on Rusty as I moved around to his side and put my good leg in the stirrup. But I couldn't push off with my right leg and came down with a thump. A silent scream ripped through my body.

"Try again," Kestrel said, her voice frantic. I did, and she shoved me upward as soon as I was off the ground. I slumped across Rusty's back and then was astride. Seconds later, Kestrel was on Twitchy's back and we were off, galloping through the snow, leaving the wolf behind to be nothing more than a dark smear against the trees. The only thing that caught us was its howl, full of frustration and loss as the cry rose and swelled around us, vibrating through our blood, echoing in our bones.

Twilight knew something was wrong when we got back to the barn. I don't think she could smell the wolf on us, because it didn't touch any of us, but it had somehow left its mark. Maybe it was the fear that still hung around us like a shroud. Or our movement, still quick and shaky with adrenalin.

I slid carefully from Rusty's back and landed as gently as possible on my sore leg. I was already feeling better, so I figured there'd been no permanent damage – or any reason to tell Mom. It sure hurt as my pants rubbed against it though, and I knew that by tomorrow I'd have the biggest bruise of my life. So far, anyway.

"Can I see it?" Kestrel asked, when I sat down on a bale of hay.

"Sure." I rolled up my pant leg. Okay, so I was being optimistic when I said the bruise wouldn't arrive until tomorrow. It bloomed dark and purple across my upper shin, just below my knee.

"Ouch," said Kestrel.

"Yeah, ouch. And it's going to get worse. Mom might even notice it."

"Just keep it covered," said Kestrel. "Oh, and don't limp."

"No prob," I said, being just a little sarcastic. I stood and stepped out. Then I paused, took another step. And repeated. And repeated. Actually, it wasn't hurting as much now. Maybe I *could* walk without a limp, as long as I concentrated. I moved slowly to Twilight's stall, continuing to practice a normal walk. She glared at me over the door, backing when I got closer. I walked back to Rusty.

"That's pretty good," said Kestrel. "Do you want help untacking?"

"No, I can do it."

Kestrel moved to unsaddle Twitchy and I did the same with Rusty. They deserved tons of oats tonight, after what we'd put them through. "So tomorrow, we should take them a bit more food," I said, "before you have to head home again,"

Kestrel looked at me, her expression incredulous. "You want to go back there? After what happened? I can't believe you – it's like you have a death wish or something."

"We can't just let them die."

"Oh yeah, the poor wolves. Why don't we just feed them one of us?"

"You don't have to come." I pulled Rusty's saddle from his back and carried it toward the tack room. The stirrup banged against my sore leg, making tears pop out.

"I'm supposed to let you go by yourself?" Now she sounded even more unbelieving.

I scowled and spun around. "Well, if you won't come and you won't stay…" I stopped. A wide grin stretched across Kestrel's face. She'd just been teasing me? A small smile touched my own lips despite my best intentions. "Brat!"

Kestrel just laughed and turned back to Twitchy.

"So glad I can amuse you." I continued on to the tack room.

We finished putting our gear away, then groomed the horses until they shone in the lantern light. After Rusty, Twitchy, and Cocoa dove into their suppers, Kestrel and I went into Twilight's stall, and though she laid her ears back at us she still stood for us to brush her. Then we gave her some more hay and fresh grain, even though she still hadn't touched the old grain in her bucket.

"So seriously, how are we going to help the wolves and stay safe?" Kestrel asked on the way to the house. Loonie came out to meet us.

"I think if one of us climbs and the other stays with the horses, we'll be okay."

"So what if the one with the horses has to get them out of there? We can't leave the climber behind."

I frowned. "No. That's not good."

"Maybe we should try riding the horses nearer the den. We can find the back way that the wolf used today."

"That's a good idea." I paused at the door. "By the way, thanks for saving me today. From falling and, well, everything."

Kestrel smiled. "Anytime."

Mom put down her paintbrush when Kestrel and I entered the cabin. "Where have you two been? I was getting worried."

"Just for a ride, Mom." I tried not to wince as I pulled my boot off.

"Why didn't you take Loonie?"

I scratched the old dog behind her ear. "She doesn't come with us much anymore. Most of the time she just goes as far as the trees and then turns around."

"Poor old girl," Mom said, and sighed. Her voice brightened as she continued. "So I was thinking, since I made you girls cookies today, maybe you could return the favor by cooking dinner."

"That sounds fun," said Kestrel, though I knew she had no idea how to cook.

"You'll eat whatever we make?" I asked, just to double-check that mom knew what she was getting into.

"If you can eat it, I can eat it," she said as she continued to put away her paints.

Kestrel elbowed me. "Look at that," she whispered and pointed to Mom's painting. Even in the meager lantern light, the painting made me breathless. I couldn't believe how much Mom had improved since she'd seen the horses dancing in the meadow. It was as if that night had awakened something wild and beautiful inside her soul.

"I want that painting," said Kestrel.

Mom laughed nervously. "It's not finished yet," she said and turned the painting against the wall.

"It's amazing, Mom," I said. "Really. We're not joking."

"Well, we'll see what Edward thinks of it. He may say it's overly dramatic."

Kestrel and I looked at each other. Mom was so wrong. The painting was fantastic, even though this one didn't have mustangs in it. It was simply a landscape of a snowy field and trees and distant mountains, but at the same time, it was so much more.

Looking into that painting you could feel the bite of frost on your cheeks, and the cold air in your lungs. You could imagine running into that pure whiteness and flopping down and making snow angels and rolling in the snow and laughing until you didn't have the breath to laugh any more. You could imagine lying on your back and gazing into that cerulean sky and watching the evening come on and the stars appearing one by one. You could imagine falling in love there. It was magic. Pure and simple. And my mom had done it.

The next day, we wolfed – no pun intended – down a big breakfast, and then changed Twilight's bandage. She fought us even more than the day before. Two hours later, the bandage was changed and Kestrel and I were as sick of Twilight as she was of us.

As we rode away across the meadow, I was relieved that Mom still hadn't discovered that we'd taken the jerky, even though it was just a matter of time. She would have known by now if she hadn't asked us to make dinner last night. We'd been amazingly lucky.

When we were about halfway across the meadow, Mom let Loonie out of the barn where we'd left her. The old girl came bounding after us, joy suffusing her entire canine face. I hardly had the heart to turn her back after we entered the trees and Mom couldn't hear me tell her to go home, but I had to do it. It was too dangerous for Loonie to be around the wolves. I silently promised her that I'd take her with me that afternoon, when I rode Kestrel halfway home.

Once at the bluff, it took a while to make sense of the wolves' tracks, or rather, non-tracks. We'd hoped to follow them through the wolves' back door, but there'd been a light skiff of snow overnight and all we could see were indentations here and there – impossible to tell if they were former tracks or indents left by tiny snow chunks falling from trees or whatever. We tried to find the den by riding in its general direction, but it was well hidden and we kept missing it.

"I'm going to have to go pretty soon," Kestrel finally said, after our sixth unsuccessful pass.

"Okay, I'll just climb the bluff. You can wait below with the horses, okay?"

"You promise you'll be careful?"

"I promise."

"I'll be right below you."

The climb up was relatively quick compared to the night before. Slowly, I raised my head above the lip of the bluff and looked down toward the den. Only the black hole was there. No sign of the wolves. I raised higher. Still no wolves. The fresh snow in front of the den was unbroken. Nothing had passed over its surface since the snow had fallen last night.

I looked down at Kestrel and gave her a wave, then hoisted myself over the lip of the bluff.

"Evy, what are you doing?"

I looked back and waved, then put my finger to my lips.

The snow crunched as I moved closer to the den, the bag of moose jerky over my shoulder. No point in dumping it unless the wolves were still living in the den. Our investigation yesterday may have made them move on and if they were gone, I wanted to sneak the meat back into the smokehouse.

I crept even closer, and with every step became more confident that there was no one home. At the mouth of the den, I bent down to peer inside. It wasn't much of a den, being more like a shallow dirt dugout. And it was empty. Though it was well hidden, it wouldn't have been a comfortable home for them. In fact, I was surprised they'd denned here at all, especially during the coldest weather. No wonder they'd been having trouble.

"Evy! What are you doing?"

I turned around. Kestrel was climbing over the ridge, her eyes wild. She must have tied up the horses and climbed it in record time. "They're gone," I said. "I was just double-checking."

The tight expression on her face increased. "You could have told me they were gone."

"Sorry. When I signaled you, I just *thought* they might be gone, and didn't want to startle them if they were still here."

"And what if they *were* still here? They could have killed you."

"But they weren't," I repeated and turned back to the den. Why was Kestrel harassing me? She wasn't my mom.

The silence behind me grew increasingly pointed and brittle, but I had practice at ignoring problems – I am my mother's daughter, after all – so I hummed and faked a long visual search of the den, which told me nothing that I hadn't already figured out. When I finally felt able to face Kestrel, I arranged an apologetic expression on my face and turned around.

She was gone.

I hurried to the edge of the bluff. She was already halfway down, and I could tell she was upset by the way she moved.

"I'm sorry," I yelled, but she didn't stop.

I started down and made it close to the ground in record speed, but then slipped on an icy rock and went flying backwards. I landed in the snow on my back and stared up at the blue, blue sky. I heard snow-muffled hoofbeats, and then Twitchy's big nose came into view, with Kestrel glaring down at me.

"Are you okay?" she asked, sounding like she wished my answer was "no."

"Yeah." I sat up. "Sorry," I said again, trying my best to sound contrite. I really hate it when Kestrel gets mad at me, especially since she's my only friend – literally.

"Can you imagine what that's like? To see you walk out of sight toward three wild wolves? How would you feel if *you* were the one at the bottom of the cliff, watching *me* do something so totally stupid?"

"It's not really a cliff." Okay, I was being a little evasive.

"How would you feel?" She wasn't about to be distracted.

So I thought about it – and the unpleasant realization struck me that I would be terrified for her. "Sorry," I repeated for a third time, and this time I really meant it.

Her face lightened, just a bit. "You can be so frustrating sometimes, Evy. It's like you think you can do anything and never get hurt. What if they weren't gone? What if the big one came out of the den and attacked you?"

"Yeah, it was a mistake. I won't do it again," I said as

I climbed to my feet. One of my boots had come off and I looked around, while standing on one leg – my uninjured leg, thank goodness.

Actually, Kestrel was wrong. I didn't think I'd never get hurt. I just thought that sometimes things were worth a bit of pain, but there was no use telling her that. She really wasn't into listening right then. Instead, I'd let her have her rant and then she'd be okay. She's really great when she doesn't get all cautious and stuff. Like yesterday. She was Supergirl then, saving me from plummeting to my death and leaping off a cliff to save her horse.

I finally spied my boot and hopped to pick it up, then knocked the snow out of it.

"So do you think they left for good?" she asked, finally acting more like Super-Kestrel.

"I think so. I think we scared them away yesterday."

"So that's why the big wolf ran to attack us yesterday? Because it was scared of us?" Kestrel being sarcastic.

"Maybe after we left it realized we could come back to the den anytime, even while it was out hunting." I went to untie Rusty.

Gone, he said, when I climbed to his back.

I rolled my eyes. Nice of him to tell me now.

When we got home, we sneaked the jerky back into the smokehouse, said hi and bye to Mom, and started off toward Kestrel's house. Loonie romped beside us like a pup as Kestrel and I talked about the different techniques we'd heard for training young horses. She thought imprinting might be good for Twilight, even

though she wasn't a foal, and I wanted to be convinced
it would work. I was desperate to find some way to stop
the battles. Tonight would be my first time cleaning her
wound alone and I wasn't looking forward to it.

I waved goodbye to Kestrel at the halfway point and
turned Rusty toward home, then dove into my thoughts.
While imprinting sounded good, I wondered if it would
only make things worse. Twilight's problem wasn't
fear so much as anger. Also, though she seemed willing
enough to stand to be groomed, imprinting was a lot
more invasive: touching her everywhere, over and over.
She'd totally hate it. Just like she hated everything to do
with me and her new life – well, except for the grooming,
I guess.

Not knowing what to do was totally frustrating,
especially since I could sense Twilight's unhappiness
below the rage. She felt isolated and alone – but it almost
seemed on purpose, and that made me kind of mad at her,
even though I didn't want to be. She didn't *want* to know
we were nice. She didn't *want* to accept that we were
trying to help her. She didn't *want* to realize I'd saved
her life. She just wanted to resent us and dislike us and
escape as soon as possible.

I didn't know how to fix the problem without talking
to her – and that was something I could never, ever do.
If she ever discovered I was Willow's murderer, the slim
chance of having a relationship with her would turn into
no chance. The two had been close friends, plus they
were half sisters, and when Willow had been injured
it had devastated Twilight. She'd moped around after

the young mare, almost as if she was in mourning, as if Willow had died right then. I could only imagine how terrible it was for her when her sister really did die.

And because I didn't want Twilight to hate me forever, I could *never* speak to her. That meant I had to find another way to get her to like me, to get her to accept that I only wanted the best for her, to get her to realize that captivity wasn't that bad. There had to be a way to get her to enjoy being a domestic horse – and I hoped, to get her to like being *my* horse.

The last days of winter passed in a blur. There was so much to do. I spent a lot of time at my desk getting ahead on my homework so I could have some freedom come spring. The only other things I did were ride Rusty and spend time with Twilight: treating her wound, training her, brushing her, petting her, trying desperately to get her to like me. I kept an eye out for the wolves too, but there was no further sign of them. I hoped that meant they'd found food – food that wasn't horsemeat!

Twilight's physical condition kept getting better and better and soon she was putting weight on her leg. Then she started using it when she walked. She limped at first, but with every passing day she used it a bit more and the limp lessened. It was like her body was on overdrive to fix her leg. She certainly had access to a lot of nutrients as she healed up. She ate… well, like a horse.

Mom was worried. Every time she came down to the barn she asked how many bales were left and, every once in a while, how many bags of grain. Twilight was little so she didn't eat massive amounts of hay, though she still ate more than I would've guessed. However, she'd totally learned to love oats. She'd neigh along with the other horses when she heard the first grains rattle into the buckets and then pace until I got her bucket to her stall. It was the only time she was happy to see me. As a result, I gave her more than I should, and we were running out way too fast.

I started rationing poor Rusty and Cocoa, which Rusty thought was highly unfair and he told me so every day. I tried to make it up to him by grooming him twice a day instead of just in the morning and that helped a bit. At least he knew I still loved him. It was necessity that was making me cut back, not because Twilight was my favorite.

Twilight, on the other hand, still couldn't stand me. She stood to be groomed because I insisted and she loved the feel of it, but our training sessions were complete battles. Though she was losing the war, she never gave in. She continued to despise me, thinking her captivity was my fault. Apparently, having a wolf try to eat her was part of my master plan to trap her. She daydreamed about running away and reuniting with her herd, over and over, like a broken record.

However, as time went on, she came to like Rusty and Cocoa, even missing them during the day when they were in the pasture. She learned to like Socrates and Plato, the barn cats. The hardest time was the day I realized she liked Loonie more than she liked me. Dogs are so much like wolves – they're even a related species – and yet Twilight would rather see Loonie trotting toward her stall than me, even when I was carrying oats.

One day, in an effort to win her over, I decided to take

her out of the barn. She still wasn't leading very well, but she was getting better, following me grudgingly up and down the barn aisle when the doors were closed. She hadn't put up a serious struggle for a week now and I figured she needed a reward for her relatively good behavior.

First, I pulled back the big doors opening to the yard, making the way clear to lead her out, then entered her stall and haltered her. She was already excited and refused to stand still to be groomed. I should have taken the hint and kept her in, but it was a beautiful sunny day and I really wanted her to start associating me with good things – so I opened the stall door and led her out.

Halfway out the stall door, she jumped forward and bolted for the big doors. Automatically, I braced myself against her lead rope and she came swinging around to face me – which I quickly realized was the worst possible thing. Now she thought she had to fight me to escape. She reared up in the air and slashed out with her front hooves. I couldn't do anything but jump back. But there was no way I was going to let go of that rope!

She tried to run again and I pulled her around. This time, her desperation was clear as she fought me. For the first time, I saw doubt in her eyes – which only made her fight harder, move quicker. She lunged at me, trying to bite, and I jumped back again, into her stall this time. Again, she ran and I stopped her. This time it was easier, because I could use the inside wall of her stall for leverage.

She reared up, wild with the desire to be free, and cried out like a lost soul. Shivers coursed along my

back and Rusty answered her. I could hear his hoofbeats thudding as he raced to his stall door and found it shut.

What's happening? Rusty asked me. *What's wrong!*

She wants to run away.

She's not ready.

I won't let her go.

Not yet, said Rusty.

Not ever.

Not yet. So firm. So sure of himself.

Not ever, I replied, just as firmly.

Completely oblivious to our conversation, Twilight continued to fight the rope like the wild thing she was, pulling back with every frantic muscle, her shoulders and flanks already flecked with sweat. Air whistled through her nostrils.

Just as she went up on her hind legs again, I threw myself back against the rope, pulling her forward – and when she came down her head was through her stall door. She looked around, wide-eyed with surprise that she was back inside her stall, then screamed, reared, slashed out.

Her front hoof struck my shoulder and agony shot through my body. I would have dropped the rope, except that the pain made me a thousand times more determined that she wasn't going to escape, and I mustered every shred of will power, strength, and resolve I had left to pull her forward once again as she descended.

She froze when all four feet touched the ground, as if not believing she was actually back where she'd started – inside her stall. Taking the opportunity, I darted around her and slammed her door shut.

Anger, betrayal, sadness, and disappointment tumbled through my heart like an acrobat as I listened to Twilight rip around her stall. Her desperation, the frantic sounds, the dying hope, they all made me feel sick to my stomach. I hurried down the barn aisle, my hand on my injured shoulder. The throbbing pain kept trying to interrupt my thoughts, so I gratefully allowed the hurt to fill my mind. I stopped outside the barn. Behind me, Twilight still raced around her stall, heedless of her injury.

I knew that eventually I had to go back in there. She still had her halter and lead rope on. But for now, all I could do was stare up at the blue sky and try not to cry. *Patience, patience,* I chanted to myself. *I have to have patience. Twilight will come around in time.* Lots of people caught the wild horses and trained them until they became good saddle horses. My filly might be a little more stubborn than most, but she'd eventually adjust. I had to control my negative thoughts and give her time.

She was slowing, so I forced myself to walk back to her stall. She stopped to glare at me with hate filled eyes. I felt like an ogre, the way she looked at me.

My gaze shifted downward to her wound. It didn't need a bandage anymore, though I still cleaned it twice daily, soaking it and putting salve on it. It looked the same. She hadn't damaged her leg any more, at least.

Breathing deeply, I leaned on the stall door. What could I do to get through to her? "You're my girl, Twilight," I murmured to her. "You just don't know it yet."

After giving her more time to calm down, I'd go back

inside her stall with some oats and brushes. Then I'd take her halter off and skip the training session for the day. Tomorrow I'd open the doors again, but keep the filly in her stall. And the day after that too. Then, when she could take that much without getting too excited, I'd open one door so light could come in, but block it somehow – maybe with the wheelbarrow – and lead her up and down the barn aisle. Then, without the wheelbarrow in the way. Then with two doors open.

Step by step, that's how we'd do this. Within weeks, I'd be able to lead her outside. Then soon I'd be ponying her alongside Rusty, building up her strength and stamina.

And she *would* learn to like me... no, she'd learn to *love* me, just like Rusty. By the time I was through with her, she'd be a domestic horse in both heart and mind, hardly remembering her old ways. I just had to have patience, that's all.

The next morning, Twilight was different. She was as good as gold with the main barn door open, almost as if she didn't see the sunlight streaming past her stall. The next day was the same, so I blocked the big door with the wheelbarrow and led her out of her stall. She followed me, sedate and morose, up and down the barn aisle.

At first I felt happy. I finally had exactly what I wanted: an obedient Twilight. Yet as minutes passed, I could hardly bear to walk with her. She was far too subdued, as if the spark that was *her* was shrinking with every passing moment.

But maybe it was just my imagination. Time for a test. I moved the wheelbarrow and led her outside. She followed me with her head down and her ears loose, like an old plow horse after a hard day's work. I felt sick looking at her, so I took her back to her stall and almost ran from the barn. Loonie and Rusty got a lot of attention that day.

The next day was Kestrel's day to come visit. I led Twilight from the barn when Kestrel rode into the yard. Surprise was alive on her face when she saw us.

"Wow, Evy, she's being so good."

I smiled a half smile. "I know." I led my filly toward them as Twitchy minced around muddy patches. Kestrel kept her eyes on Twilight and I searched her expression, knowing my friend would tell me the truth. So far, so good. Then her forehead crinkled. We stopped when we met. Twitchy sniffed at Twilight as Kestrel dismounted.

"Something's different about her," said Kestrel. "It's weird, but she seems smaller than I remember."

I sagged against the filly's neck, and in my moment of hopelessness, I dropped my guard – and I felt what Twilight was feeling.

Not anger. Not fear. Not resentment.

Nothing. That's what she was feeling. Her emotions were completely blank. Being held captive had beaten down the beauty that had been hers. Twilight had become an empty shell.

All the while that she was fighting me, I held firm, but in that instant, when I realized she was giving up on life, everything changed. What right did I have to keep her? She'd hurt her leg and I'd healed her, but she didn't ask me to. Helping her had been my choice. I couldn't expect her to pay for my actions by doing something so foreign to her nature as become a domestic horse.

I had two choices. One, let her return to her home. Or two, murder two horses in her herd – both Twilight and Willow – because killing Twilight's spirit was murder.

Kestrel was staring at me and I realized I hadn't answered her last comment. I opened my mouth to speak, but nothing came out.

My friend understood immediately. She put her arms

around me in a hug. "You saved her life. She'll never forget you for that, even if she goes back to the wild ones."

I wished I could take comfort from Kestrel's words, but she didn't know that Twilight saw me as the enemy. This beautiful filly, with whom I'd fallen deeply and madly in love, would only despise me forever. Kestrel suddenly realized I was doing more than just feeling bad – I was crying – and she hugged me harder, which didn't help at all.

When my sniffling turned into sobs, she turned me toward the barn. She knew I wouldn't want Mom to see me like this. The two horses walked placidly behind us, one happy that her day's work was over, and the other, reluctant. Broken.

When I could talk, Kestrel and I made plans in quiet voices. Before we let Twilight go, she needed to become stronger. Plus we thought it would be good if there was grass for her to eat once she returned to the wild. One month, that would be long enough for her to finish healing. It would allow time for the rest of the snow to melt. Last year's grass would be uncovered and shortly after, new grass would be growing.

All the while, Twilight stood with her head to her knees, watching us with dull eyes. I almost wished to see that spark of hatred again.

When the plans were finally made, I cried a bit more, and then as soon as my eyes weren't too red, Kestrel and I headed up to the cabin. Being around Twilight only made me feel worse.

As the days passed, Twilight continued to be

depressed and dull about everything. I had a hard time getting her to eat and it was good that she didn't have competition for her food, because she even lost her gusto for oats. The hay itself, much of the time, looked untouched in the mornings. She started losing weight.

There were some good things for her too though. Socrates and Plato started sleeping in her stall after she became resigned to what she thought her fate. After a couple of lessons about the fence, she was allowed to go out with Rusty and Cocoa and the three of them seemed to enjoy each other's company. However, her favorite thing was to go on excursions with Rusty and me – okay, with Rusty. From her point of view, I just happened to be there too. But that was when I'd see her almost happy. When Rusty was ready to go and I was walking toward her stall with her lead rope and halter, she wouldn't hunch up as if pained.

Two weeks after the decision had been made, on the day that Kestrel normally came to visit, I asked Mom if I could go to meet Kestrel a bit early – actually ride to her house and visit there for a few minutes before heading back home. Her older sisters were always nice to me, and her dad was always teasing her mom, which was fun to watch. I had another motive different from watching family bonding, though – I thought it would be good for Twilight. She would get some exercise, plus she might feel less depressed if she spent more time out of her stall.

I went out to saddle Rusty just as the day was breaking. If I wanted to catch Kestrel before she left her house, we'd have to leave early. By the time we left the barn, the sun was just above the horizon, a round red ball. I waved goodbye to Mom as I passed the window. She was already painting up a storm. I couldn't believe the number of paintings she'd finished over the last couple of months – five or six now. And they'd been getting more abstract and impressive and amazing all the while. Edward was going to be thrilled when he came this spring.

We'd made out our supply list last night, Mom and I, telling him what to buy with the proceeds of her sales since last fall. The letter was now in an envelope in my saddlebag. Kestrel and her family always mailed letters for us, since Mom never went into town. They also received letters for us: Edward's letters for Mom, and for me, three secret pen pals. I didn't feel too guilty about it – a girl needs some contact with the outside world – and had a letter ready to send to my Vancouver pen pal, Ally, in my saddlebag.

The land lay quiet as we strode along. It felt great to be riding toward Kestrel's house. I hadn't seen any sort of civilization for almost four months and the thought of seeing the big ranch house at Kestrel's, the big barns, basically any large human-made structure, seemed totally exciting. I hoped we'd have time to hang out in Kestrel's room for a while. She had posters all over her walls and the walls themselves are bright green and not plain logs like in our cabin. And she had her own room. She didn't even share with her sisters. Just with her fat cat, Snarly, named for the tooth that angled out of his upper jaw and held his lip up. He was always fluffed at the foot of her bed, a big pile of tangled fur with a permanently grumpy face.

I asked Rusty to go faster and he moved into a ground-eating trot. Twilight loped alongside, keeping the lead rope loose. The birds shrieked around us, ecstatic that the winter was almost over. The earliest spring birds were back, and they flung their little bodies from branch to branch. I inhaled deeply, imagining I was drawing in birdsong with each breath. What a great morning to be out with my two lovely horses – no, my one lovely horse and the wild one… In two weeks, Twilight would be gone.

I glanced down at the filly. She loped along with her head up and ears forward. She was enjoying the excursion as well. Maybe I could keep her after all? No! I'd already made that decision. It was best for her to be free, and I had to do what was best for her.

But what if she was now, finally and belatedly, getting used to captivity? What if she did regain some of that precious *Twilight-ness* and was able to keep it, even as a domestic horse? Maybe she'd just needed a bit more time to adjust. Okay, a *lot* more. But still, maybe she was adjusting.

Rusty stopped short, Twilight beside him. Had he heard my thoughts? Instantly shame colored my face. But he was looking through the trees to the right of the rutted road, his ears pricked forward.

I didn't want to ask him what he noticed in case Twilight overheard our communication, so I simply encouraged him to walk on, thinking he'd want to investigate whatever it was. I was right. He headed into the trees. Twilight dropped behind him so she could follow as he wound his way among the tree trunks. I ducked low over his back and peered ahead. A natural meadow appeared through the forest, small, ordinary, and a bit wet because of all the snowmelt. Then I saw the small band of horses.

I pulled Rusty to a stop and slid from his back, then put my hand over his nose so he'd know to be quiet. Twilight hadn't seen them yet, thank goodness.

I tied Rusty to a tree and Twilight right beside him so that Rusty's big gray body was between her and the distant horses. It was the only thing I could do other than ride away, and I really didn't want to do that. They could be wild horses. Rusty seemed to know what to do and stood stoically between Twilight and the glimpses of meadow.

Quickly, I moved through the trees toward them. The going was easy because there was no snow and the twigs were too soggy to snap. As long as I didn't rustle any bushes and stayed hidden, the horses wouldn't know I was there. Every few seconds, I'd stop to watch them and the closer I got, the more certain I became that they were wild horses. I couldn't see any brands.

Then everything started happening at once. Twilight's plaintive neigh rang out – she'd seen them! I could hear her mad struggles and Rusty calling me. The wild horses spooked across the meadow and were about to thunder into the trees on the other side, when Twilight neighed again – and a sorrel mare broke from the herd and stopped. The others disappeared into the trees, but the mare didn't follow. She held her head high and her answering neigh echoed across the meadow. Then she trotted toward us. The way she moved seemed so familiar and I wondered where I'd seen her before. The sun glimmered on her rough coat and I could see the patches where she'd been shedding. Then I recognized the star on her forehead, jagging toward her right eye.

Willow.

But how could she be here? She was dead.

Slowly, I stood to face her. The mare saw me and stopped short, staring in horror. Then quick as breath, she wheeled away and ran. I followed her without thinking, dashing around tree trunks and leaping over obstructions. I entered the meadow just before she disappeared into the trees on the other side. It was Willow, for sure. Not just her identical star and similar appearance – she was just shaggy and older now – but the fact she came to Twilight's call. She'd remembered her sister and friend.

A tremendous lightness suffused me as I turned back to Twilight and Rusty. I wasn't a murderer! I hadn't caused Willow's death! She just lived with another herd now. Maybe the rival stallion that had fought with Night Hawk before the cold snap had stolen her. And she hadn't limped as she trotted across the meadow toward us. I hadn't even maimed her. She'd just needed time to heal.

Twilight's scream brought me to my senses and a sudden, dreadful abandonment slammed into me. I shoved it into the back room of my mind, but not before tears of longing studded my eyes. Poor Twilight! She wanted to follow Willow so badly that she was beyond reason. She called again and again as I hurried back to her. She was straining against her rope and staring past me at the meadow as I approached her and Rusty. She

hardly noticed when I touched her neck and stroked her. She neighed again and again.

Kestrel's call came from the road. "Who's there? What's wrong?"

"It's me," I called. "I need help."

Even with Kestrel's help, it took all our strength to untie Twilight's rope once she stopped pulling. As we rode back toward our cabin, the filly jerked against the rope again and again, hoping against hope that somehow she'd find herself free to follow Willow. Kestrel and I rode in silence. It was too hard to converse when we had the filly fighting us every step of the way, calling out over and over for a friend long gone.

I was glad we couldn't talk much. I couldn't really tell Kestrel the things in my heart, as I'd never said anything about murdering Willow. She'd never understand the complete and total relief that overwhelmed me at finding the mare well and healthy. And besides, I was worried about what she'd say if we started talking. I could feel her thinking that I should turn Twilight loose right then, and in a way, it would have been a good solution. Twilight could always join Willow's herd.

But I couldn't release her yet. There were things to explain to Twilight, now that I was free to talk to her. I needed to tell her that I'd *saved* her life, that I *wasn't* a monster. I needed her to know I *wasn't* trying to hurt her when I cleaned her wound.

And I needed to tell her that I loved her.

Maybe then, with the silence broken, she would see she'd misjudged me. Maybe then she'd love me back.

My chance came that evening when, for some bizarre reason, Mom left off her painting early and started talking to us. She wanted news of the outside world and asked Kestrel question after question. I wasn't sure what brought on her unusual interest, but I wasn't going to complain, not when it gave me a chance to spend some time alone with Twilight.

"I'm going to check on the horses. Be back in a minute," I said quietly, and made a quick exit before Kestrel could finish saying something excruciatingly dull to Mom. I could almost feel her protest pulling me back and totally felt sorry for her. Talking to adults is like taking tests. They ask the most boring questions. "Let's play cards when I get back, okay?" I said as a way to make it up to her.

"Sure," Mom said brightly and the cornered expression on Kestrel's face lightened a bit. She liked card games.

The barn was serene in the lamplight, the horses drowsy inside their stalls, and Socrates and Plato snug in front of the stove. The only sound was the click of Loonie's toenails as she followed me across the wooden floor. I moved to Twilight's stall door and leaned over it.

She was curled up in the hay, facing the corner. I bowed my head before the sadness oozing out of her. I had let this go on for far too long. If only I'd known about Willow sooner, or been braver about facing rejection – a rejection that came anyway.

Twilight?

The filly's head shot up. She scrambled to her hooves and stared at me, wild eyed. Obviously, there wasn't going to be an easy way to do this.

Twilight, I am Evy.

She backed until her hindquarters were in the far corner. I waited until she calmed a bit, then spoke again. *I wanted to help you when I brought you here. I wanted to make you well and strong.*

No words, but impressions came to my mind. She didn't see me as making her well and strong. I was the one who hurt her everyday.

Tears prickled my eyes. *I did not want to hurt you. I cleaned the wound that the wolf made. You needed that to heal. And now, you are strong. But I'm sorry I hurt you to heal you.*

All I got in return was a feeling of confusion. She didn't really understand what I was saying. Too many words, probably. I closed my eyes and offered an image to her – her wound and me cleaning it and the wound looking better after cleaning. Then like time-lapse photography, showing it getting better and better. In response, the confusion changed to a stubborn resolve. She wasn't about to give me credit for helping her. In her mind, her body had healed itself, in spite of my actions.

I didn't know what to say or think, so I just looked at her as she glared at me. This was certainly the way to get her stubborn *Twilightness* back – start an argument with her.

Home. Now. Her first words were loud and forceful in my mind, making me step backward. She wanted me to release her this second.

Tomorrow. Why did I say that? It was two weeks earlier than planned. But she wanted it so desperately. How could I make her wait that long when she was basically well? Another great silence stretched between us, as if she wasn't sure what she'd heard.

Tomorrow we find your herd. You go back to them, I repeated.

Another big silence.

I would never hurt you. I looked down at the ground. *I love you.*

Seconds stretched to a full minute as I waited for her response. It didn't come in words, but actions. She turned her hindquarters toward me, lowered her head, and hunched her back. She was telling me to get lost. She didn't believe me.

I fought for clarity as emotions rocketed through my mind and body. It was so clear that Twilight would never trust me. She'd never love me. I was only her captor, that's all, and would never be anything else. Talking to her had made no difference.

I am sorry. I did not mean to hurt you.

What else could I say? Nothing. She saw her sire and dam as saving her from the wolf. I'd just been the one who came along afterward and separated her from them. I was the one who'd put her through daily tortures.

I ran to the barn doors and leaned there for a moment, aching to go back to Rusty's stall and seek comfort from him. But I'd see Twilight from there and I couldn't bear to look at her right now. I already hurt too much.

Loonie came up behind me and whined. I spun around and dropped to my knees. The old dog looked like she needed a hug. Oh, who am I kidding? I needed the hug. I lay my head on her fur and put my arms around her. "She hates me, Loonie."

Loonie whined and licked my hand. She loved me. So did Rusty and Cocoa, Socrates and Plato, and, of course, my mom. I was lucky. I had a great friend. I lived in a beautiful part of the world. I even had a big mystery to solve with figuring out why Mom was hiding out in the bush and about who might be looking for her – or us. I sniffled into Loonie's shoulder. I wouldn't have thought it a good thing on any other day, but today I felt safe knowing that lifelong puzzles were still in place. Except for Twilight hating me forever, everything else in my life was the same as it always had been.

Twilight does not understand, Rusty said. Comfort and warm wishes grew thick around me. *She is wrong. Someday she may see you truthfully.*

I sniffled and wiped my eyes. *Thanks, Rusty.*

Slowly, I stood. Twilight hated me. So be it. I didn't regret telling her the truth about loving her and I certainly didn't regret saving her life, even if she didn't acknowledge it. Let her give the credit to her sire and

137

dam. They had been the ones who chased off the wolf anyway.

"Thanks to you too, Loonie," I whispered. "I'm ready to go inside now."

Mom and Kestrel both looked up when I opened the door to the cabin, then Kestrel looked guiltily down at the table. As I bent to take off my boots, I wondered if they'd been talking about me. My suspicions were confirmed when Mom jumped up and said she was going to make chocolate cake with chocolate mint icing for desert. My favorite that she usually only makes on my birthday. I looked searchingly at Kestrel. What had they been saying?

Mom was still prattling on about the cake when I sat at the table. "What were you talking about?" I mouthed to Kestrel.

"She didn't know you were freeing Twilight," she whispered.

I squeezed my eyes shut in relief. Now I didn't have to tell Mom myself. "Tomorrow," I whispered back.

Kestrel's eyes widened. "Tomorrow?"

I nodded, then got up from the table and went into the bedroom, shutting the door behind me. I heard the murmur of voices on the other side of the door. Kestrel was probably telling Mom my plans. Then the other room became quiet. A soft knock sounded on the bedroom door. When I didn't answer, it opened.

"Evy? Are you okay?" Kestrel asked.

I covered my face with my pillow in an attempt to hide the tears that had started once again. I felt her sit on my bed.

"Sorry about telling. I just wanted to make it easier for you."

I tried to say it was okay, but for a moment, couldn't speak. Sorrow at losing Twilight stuck in my throat. I felt so helpless, so full of grief – and then I forced myself to remember that she'd never been mine. I thought of how excited she'd be tomorrow, to be going home, and that helped me find my strength again. I looked up from the pillow.

"It's okay. I'm not mad. Just sad." I sniffled and tried to smile.

Somehow I made it through the evening. We played cards and then Mom and Kestrel played a game of chess while I stared out the window – and finally it was bedtime. Kestrel and I settled in the front room like we always do when she stays over.

"I'm sorry, Evy," she said, as soon as Mom was gone to the bedroom.

"It's okay. Really," I said, trying to sound more convincing. "I don't know how I could've told her."

That seemed to satisfy her, because she moved on to another topic. "You got a letter from your pen pal in Vancouver." I heard the rustle of paper as she pulled the envelope from her backpack. "It feels stiff, like it has photos in it."

"I'll open it tomorrow, okay?" I turned over and pulled the sleeping bag up to my chin.

Paper crinkled as Kestrel put the envelope back in her backpack. There was a long silence, then a soft, "Good-night."

"Good-night."

Of course, I couldn't sleep. After I was sure Kestrel was asleep, I let Loonie inside and curled up in the big chair by the window. The old girl settled at my feet as I stared into the darkness.

There was no moon and the night was as black as it could get. When I finally shut my eyes it looked the same behind my eyelids, the dark endless, the night eternal. This night was the last night Twilight slept in my barn. I imagined her there, wondering if she really would be going home tomorrow, her hope battling her unwillingness to believe anything good of me.

In one way, she'd be dreading the morning, thinking I'd lied to her. And yet I had no doubt that some small part of her would be wishing the night away, just as I wanted to hold it back. And neither of us could affect it at all because the night is what it is. The world is what it is. Life is what it is.

All we can do is the best we can and let others be who they are. Twilight was wild. I had to accept that.

When I woke, the sun warmed my skin through the window and spring smell saturated the air, even inside the cabin. Loonie was gone. I looked for her and saw Kestrel reading a book in her sleeping bag.

"Hey," I said.

She looked up from her book. "Hey."

I dropped my voice so Mom wouldn't hear. "You put Loonie outside?"

Mom lurched half asleep into the room. Kestrel quickly nodded as Mom staggered to the kitchen, picked up the coffeepot that she'd prepared the night before, and put it on the stove. A massive yawn split her face. She's kind of touchy first thing in the morning and wouldn't have been too pleased to find Loonie inside the house. I owed Kestrel yet another one.

We quickly fed the horses and had breakfast ourselves, then headed back to the barn. For the first time in ages, Twilight was out of her corner, waiting both grumpily and eagerly by the stall door. She stamped when I was too slow putting on her halter and then kept tugging on her lead rope as I was saddling Rusty. She was so impatient to leave that she didn't even answer Cocoa's neigh as we left the barn.

"So where do we go?" asked Kestrel.

Grass Lake, thought Rusty.

I repeated his thought aloud, and we were off.

As we rode, I hoped and prayed with all my strength that the mustangs wouldn't be there. Twilight's release could be postponed, maybe for weeks, if her herd wasn't in our area.

"Mya gave me her gold stud earrings," said Kestrel. Mya is Kestrel's oldest sister, the one who's planning on leaving for university next fall.

"Cool," I said, trying to sound enthused, and knowing Kestrel was just trying to distract me from what we had to do today.

"Mom said I could get my ears pierced the next time we go to Williams Lake."

"Cool." Twilight's conflict vibrated through me, making it hard to listen to Kestrel. But I didn't want to shut the filly out – this was the last time I'd hear her thoughts.

"That's a lot better than the way Mya got her ears pierced. She didn't want to wait until we went to Williams Lake, so she did it herself."

"Um, yeah."

"First, she sterilized a big fat needle and then froze her earlobes with ice cubes and then… Evy, are you listening to me?"

"Yeah. Sorry." How sad that Twilight kept trying to squish down her feeble hope that I would let her free.

"And then she poked the needle through."

And yet how she ached to gallop away from me, to

never see me again, to completely eliminate me from her life and thoughts. "It sounds gross," I said aloud.

"That's not even the gross part. That came when she took the needle out."

"Hmmm." If only she'd given me a chance. That's all I'd wanted. All I could have asked for.

"And put a sausage through her ear."

"Yeah." But there was nothing more I could do or say to convince her I'd healed her, not hurt her.

"Okay, so now I *know* you're not listening."

"What? I was listening. You said, um… you said something about sausages?"

Kestrel laughed. "Never mind."

Near, said Rusty. He stopped and Twilight stopped beside him, every muscle alive with anticipation. She hadn't sensed them yet.

"What's wrong? Are they close?"

I nodded my head, unable to speak.

"Where?" whispered Kestrel.

Where? I asked Rusty.

To the right. He stepped out again.

"Rusty knows which way," I explained to Kestrel.

We'd only ridden thirty seconds when Twilight sensed her family. She charged forward, then hit the end of the lead rope and was flung around to face us. I stopped Rusty and pulled her toward me. Her despair plunged over me. But not surprise. She'd expected me to stop her. She knew without a doubt that I'd wanted to torture her further.

Take ropes off first, I said, but she wasn't listening.

"Is she okay?"

"Yeah. She just knows they're there." I swung out of Rusty's saddle.

"Are you going to turn her loose here?"

I nodded. And that's what I did. I simply unbuckled her halter and let the leather slip from her head. At first she froze, as if she couldn't believe I'd actually done it, and then she was running away from us, kicking up mud like a racecar. Not a word of goodbye. Nothing.

I scrambled back into Rusty's saddle, and then Kestrel and I were off in silent pursuit. The trees whipped by to our left and right – and then Rusty slowed. I signaled to Kestrel to slow Twitchy as Twilight's rump disappeared over a hill in front of us.

Rusty stopped at the top of the hill. I searched the trees before us with frantic eyes. When I saw Twilight, she was already down the gentle slope and had just reached the lake. On the other side, eating last year's grass, was her herd. Silently, I pointed them out to Kestrel.

Twilight's high-pitched neigh rang across the water and, like quail, the mustangs scattered. Within seconds, they were all in the forest – except one. Wind Dancer. She stood like stone, and then ran toward Twilight, snuffling loudly.

They met halfway around the lake, sniffed at each other and squealed, then, far too swiftly, they galloped into the forest.

I let out my breath in a rush.

"Wow," said Kestrel. "That was quick." She sounded disappointed.

Goodbye, Twilight! I mind-called after her.

Goodbye, Twilight, said Rusty.

Goodbye, I tried again. But there was no response.

"They even know Twilight and they're still like scared rabbits," Kestrel said, shaking my concentration.

I only wanted to help you. The thought flew after the filly and bounced off her joy.

"Evy? Are you okay?"

"That's how they've survived for so long, I guess," I said, with a shaky voice. "The herds have been here for more than two hundred years."

"It's so awesome that you helped her. You saved Twilight's life and now she'll grow up to have wild babies. A whole line of mustangs will exist because of you, Evy."

Even with Kestrel trying to cheer me up, the ride back to the cabin was almost unbearable. Then, minutes after we got back to the barn, Kestrel said goodbye and took off for home, and I felt even worse. I took care of Rusty, but couldn't stand being in the same barn as Twilight's empty stall, so I went into the cabin, shut the bedroom door, and crawled into bed.

At suppertime, Mom insisted that I come out to eat, and then that I go take care of Rusty and Cocoa for the night. She said it would make me feel better, and it did as long as I kept my eyes to the one side of the barn. Right after, I went back to bed, feeling Twilight's loss like a chunk ripped out of my heart.

That night, Mom came into the room and tried to get me to talk. She said she planned to spend more time with me and that she was sorry she'd been neglecting me – as if that was the problem. I told her not to worry about it, but she didn't really listen, and started listing all the things we'd do together.

When she finally blew out her lamp, I stared out the window. This night was cloudy too and I couldn't see any stars. I stared out the window as I lay waiting for sleep, hoping to see Twilight appear there, nosing my window with an uplifted head. Pure fantasy, and I knew that. My hope was long dead.

Eventually I closed my burning eyes, dry from too many tears. Doing the right thing really stinks sometimes. If I could just sleep, then the worst day of my life would finally be over. Tomorrow had to be better. It couldn't get any worse, anyway.

Something is there, hidden in the dark of night, though I can't see it, can't smell it. But I can sense the twitching of its muscles as it prepares to attack. I can feel its desire to sink its teeth into me. It's there as sure as I am breathing.

I long to run – but I can't. I force myself to step forward into the black, the dark tree trunks the palest thing around – and behind one of them, the wolf. My heart is like a grouse beating its wings, faster and faster. My body shakes like ripples in water.

I woke from the nightmare with a huge effort, and then everything became infinitely more terrifying because the feeling didn't stop. This was no nightmare. I was already awake. Though my eyes were staring at the inside of my bedroom window, I could see tree trunks still, superimposed over the dark of the room. I was sensing a mustang being stalked by the wolf.

I forced the fear to the back of my mind – so difficult because I was half asleep – then swiftly dressed. Mom was invisible in the darkness, so I was sure she couldn't see me. She'd think I was just restless in my sleep, if she heard me at all.

Step forward. Be strong. Be brave. Step forward.

I had to get out there, right now. But what about Mom and the promise I'd made her that I'd wake her before heading out at night again?

But things were different from when I'd made that promise. Spring was here. I wouldn't freeze to death in the cold and snow, though a wolf might attack me. That was the same. I brutally shoved the thought down. I'd be safe if Loonie was with me. No need to wake Mom and her thousands of questions.

I crept to the front door and put on a warm jacket and boots, then opened the door and slipped outside. Loonie whined from her bed on the porch.

"Come on, girl. Let's go."

We ran across the meadow in the direction I could still hear the mustang's thoughts. Twilight's thoughts. But it couldn't be Twilight. That made no sense at all. She'd been longing to escape me for months. And now she was coming back? Alone? I needed to recheck my sensors.

I entered the trees and called Loonie to my side. The last thing I wanted was her rushing forward without me to back her up. I felt a warm tongue lick my fingers and smiled as I felt my way through the trees. "Good, girl. Now stay with me. Ow." A stick from a tree poked me in the neck. That was going to leave a hard-to-explain mark. Great.

We continued forward as quickly as I could, which wasn't very fast at all, on and on through the darkness. And then Loonie wasn't there. I'm not sure what tipped me off as it was too dark to see, but she just *felt* gone.

Then barking came from ahead. The mustang's relief washed over me.

"Loonie!"

I rushed forward.

A roaring growl rumbled in front of me and I stopped short. "Loonie! Loonie!"

There was a scuffling sound, and then I heard Loonie running toward me. I knelt and patted her all over, felt for injuries, felt for blood, felt for broken bones or ripped tendons – but she seemed fine. The wolf must have left without a fight. A good sign. It and its puppies must no longer be desperate and starving. I bowed my head over my brave, old dog. "Oh, Loonie, I'm so glad you're okay," I murmured, pulling her into a hug.

Then something touched my back, a tentative touch, lasting mere moments. I knew instantly who it was.

I hadn't been mistaken.

Twilight.

I could hardly breathe as I turned around. A dark form stood there. Yearling sized. Twilight shaped.

Hello, human. She thought the words hesitantly, experimenting with language.

Evy. I am Evy.

She snorted. *Funny.*

I couldn't smother my laugh and Twilight stepped back at the sound. Silence stretched between us.

Why are you here? I finally asked.

At first she didn't reply and I imagined her staring off into the darkness as she thought of the answer. *You spoke truth. You gave freedom.*

I waited for more, but there wasn't any. Twilight wasn't a big talker.

So why *did you come back?*

You spoke truth. She sounded impatient with the stupid human. But I didn't get it. My keeping my word in setting her free made her change her mind?

Then I started to understand – I'm slow, I know. Because I'd set her free, Twilight realized that everything else I'd said was true too. She knew I was sorry for hurting her. She knew I was only trying to help her.

She knew I was telling the truth when I said I loved her. And now she saw me, and everything that had happened to her, differently.

Back to stay? I thought again, hoping against hope.

No. Another long pause. *Maybe.*

My throat swelled with emotion. "Welcome home," I managed to stutter. *Happy you came back.* I reached out to see if she was close enough to touch and my fingers slid across her warm neck. I scratched her under her mane. *Welcome home,* I repeated. Twilight hesitated, then moved closer.

When the three of us started back to the barn, I felt I was walking in a dream. To have her *want* to stay with us, well, I just didn't know what to think. In a way, it made no sense and was completely unbelievable. And yet, in another way, it made all the sense in the world. Love was what mattered. And while Twilight no doubt didn't love me, she was intrigued by my love for her – and she trusted me enough to come back to investigate it further.

Stepping out from under the trees, the night became brighter. The barn loomed closer and closer and I waited for Twilight to change her mind. She didn't falter. Rusty welcomed her with a neigh and the sound woke Cocoa. I heard the scrape of her hooves on the floor as I lit the lantern in the barn, then she nickered over her door to Twilight. After Twilight gave her own greeting in return, I opened her stall door and she walked inside like royalty.

Oats, please. So maybe I added the *please* here to make her sound more polite, but I was glad to fetch them for my extremely independent and strange new horse. Well, not *my* new horse, as in ownership. No one owned Twilight but herself. She'd made that abundantly clear. So maybe it's more accurate to say, my new friend.

And as I hustled off to do her Highness's bidding and bring her a big helping of oats, I felt a warm glow. Living with Twilight was going to be a challenge for sure – but with her beside Rusty and me, there would be one other "for sure" too: completely amazing future adventures.

Maybe she'd even help me figure out Mom's big secret. I could hardly wait to get started!